WALTZING WITH THE DEAD

WALTZING WITH THE DEAD

Poems & Stories

Russell Davis

WILDSIDE PRESS
Doylestown, Pennsylvania

Copyright © 2003 Russell Davis.

ACKNOWLEDGMENTS

Sacrifices — originally published in *New Amazons* (DAW Books), 2000

One Tree Hill — originally published in *Warrior Princesses* (DAW Books), 1998

Omega Time — originally published in *Sol's Children* (DAW Books), 2002

The Death of Winston Foster — originally published in *Future Crimes* (DAW Books), 1999

The Morality of Feeling Good — originally published under the name Christopher Tracy in *HEAT, Volume 1* (Foggy Windows Books), 2001

The End of Summer — originally published in *Merlin* (DAW Books), 1999

Father of Shadow, Son of Light — originally published in *Knight Fantastic* (DAW Books), 2002

The Body Clock - originally published in *Alien Abductions* (DAW Books), 1999

Across Hickman's Bridge to Home — originally published in *Civil War Fantastic* (DAW Books), 2000

Dead Tired — originally published in *Black Cats & Broken Mirrors* (DAW Books), 1998

A Kiss at Midnight — originally published in *Single White Vampire Seeks Same* (DAW Books), 2001

The author would also like to gratefully acknowledge the following people:
Martin H. Greenberg, for everything from the beginning;
Larry Segriff, for putting up with all the damn phone calls;
John Helfers, for telling that damn silver ski jacket story to everyone he meets;
And Ed Gorman, the last prince in the business.

Waltzing With the Dead
A publication of
WILDSIDE PRESS
P.O. Box 301
Holicong, PA 18928-0301

www.wildsidepress.com

FIRST EDITION

*For my mother, Linda N. Davis (1947-2001),
who knew all along that I was trying to paint with words;*

*For my father, Harold V. Davis, Jr.,
who gave me Little Joe when I needed him most;*

*And for my daughter, Morgan Storm,
who continues to inspire me with her smile.*

Table of Contents

INTRODUCTION............................. 9
   BY ED GORMAN

Part One – Sacrifices

SACRIFICES: *A POEM*...................... 13
MONSTER: *A STORY*........................ 15
ONE TREE HILL *A STORY*................... 23
OMEGA TIME: *A STORY*..................... 33
SEVEN YEAR ITCH: *A STORY*................ 41

Part Two – Of Memories

OF MEMORIES: *A POEM*..................... 53
THE SLEEPERS: *A STORY*................... 55
A KISS OF FIRE: *A STORY*................. 75
THE DEATH OF WINSTON FOSTER: *A STORY*.... 81

Part Three – Traveler

TRAVELER: *A POEM*........................ 97
THE MORALITY OF FEELING GOOD: *A STORY*... 99
THE END OF SUMMER: *A STORY*.............. 113
FATHER OF SHADOW, SON OF LIGHT: *A STORY*. 139
THE BODY CLOCK: *A STORY*................. 139

Part Four — Waltzing with the Dead

WALTZING WITH THE DEAD: *A POEM* 159
ACROSS HICKMAN'S BRIDGE TO HOME: *A STORY* . . . 161
DEAD TIRED: *A STORY* 175
A KISS AT MIDNIGHT: *A STORY* 187

Introduction
Ed Gorman

I bought Russell Davis' first story which, for reasons I don't understand, is not included here. The vagaries of publishing contracts, I suppose, being the reason.

It was a damned good story, so much of a damned good story that over the ensuing months I bought a few other of his pieces. They were damned good stories, too, and you can read them right here and now if you want to skip over my introductory words, which I promise not to hold against you.

In a very short number of years, Russell has been a publisher, an editor and a writer. Not many of us in the storytelling trade get to see our business from so many different aspects. I think, in Russell's case, this has been a good thing because it gave him a perspective he might not have had otherwise. And that perspective, I believe, improved his writing.

See if you don't agree. To me, the later stories here are even better than the early ones. The style is more confident, the stories are more sharply defined, and

Russell's grip on the human dilemma is much firmer than it once was.

To see a writer start out at the level of craft Russell did — I'd sure hate for you to see my early stuff — and to then climb steadily higher with each new story . . . wow.

Somewhere there's an e-mail from a writer friend of mine asking me if there were any new and interesting writers about. I mentioned several names but concentrated on Russell because I thought — and still think — that he'll have a major career as a storyteller.

He's just too good to be ignored for much longer.

Ladies and gentlemen, and lovers of the word wherever you are . . . introducing Russell Davis.

— Ed Gorman

PART ONE
Sacrifices

Sacrifices

for Opal M. Davis

There can be no preparation —
to sit, stand, or pace will not
make this moment of cancer cell
knowledge more bearable. Staring
at light-motes on windows, or
shadow stars on the bedroom ceiling
will not make healing wishes true.
Prayer might help.
Family might help.
Love, or simple joy in breath —
no matter the terror crawling
with needle precision under the
delicate skin of your forearm —
these might help. There are
no guarantees, no warranty cards.
Fear might help: it will remind
you that your blood still flows,
there are still children's lunches
to be brown-bagged, matching
socks to be found, and
chemotherapy to attend.

It is possible, as all things are,
that you will lose a breast,
you may lose both.
It is possible that you will want
to run into an empty field,
scream at the sky, demand answers,
dig your nails deep into your palms
so that you bleed like a heart
on a machine shop squeeze box.
It is possible you will die.
   It is possible you will die.
      It is possible that you will live for
another 60 years not on borrowed time.
You can choose to fight, love, hate,
be angry, give of yourself to those
who see you with clear eyes.
You can be an Amazon, willing to
sacrifice now, for a chance to fight
better battles later.
This is not about dying, its
about living, choosing to live,
For 60 seconds or 60 years,
in a jungle overgrown with questions,
in a grassland plagued by storms,
in a village where the soil is rocky,
in a city, this city, where sacrifices
make real the possibles, and life is a
single, breast-beat away.

Monster

1) Medical Definition, Monster: A grossly malformed and usually nonviable fetus.
2) Medical Definition, Teratophobia: The abnormal or persistent fear of bearing a malformed child. From the Greek "teras" meaning monster and "phobos" meaning fear — literally, fear of monsters.

The two sounds had always been there. The first, a steady throbbing rhythm that cradled and comforted; the second, a melodic, sound that was higher in tone and variance than the first, but was nonetheless a pleasurable sensation.

How Tera knew these things were called "sounds" was a mystery to her — as much a mystery as knowing that she was a her, that the first sound was her mother's heartbeat, the second her mother's voice. Her knowledge of these things intruded on the sweet, liquid dreams of her growth as a fetus until she was forced to wake up. Her knowledge told her that this awakening was not normal at the same time as it explained a first concept of fairness: an unborn infant should not be aware before it is born, should not have its growth dreams and the lullabies of womb sounds broken, yet in her case it had happened — and it was decidedly unfair.

As her awareness grew, so did her knowledge, and Tera found herself able to understand information as it was presented. Sensations came, and she was aware of feeling full or hungry as the case may have been. Most of the time, unless she was hungry or uncomfortable in the tightly enclosed environment surrounding her, Tera would describe what she felt/heard/experienced as pleasurable.

Sometimes, her mother's voice would rise in song, "Singing, singing, singing, I'm singing you to sleep; singing you to slumber, gray and deep. The stars are all a shine now, the moon is in the sky; and you must drift away now; you'll dream by and by . . ." The voice would wash over her and Tera knew, unexplainable as it was, that what she felt would be called love.

For what seemed a long time, Tera floated in a happy kind of bliss; listening to her mother's voice, and another voice, deeper and more somber that she eventually learned was her father. She was warm and content, though still troubled by her unnatural awareness. There was no denying it, however, and she came to accept, even look forward to what she learned merely by listening: cars were noisy, music came from everywhere, there were other babies in the world, other animals that made loud, rough sounds when they were excited. There was so much to learn that Tera often fell asleep exhausted, overwhelmed by the input.

Had these sensations lasted forever, Tera would not have been unhappy — her environment was warm and safe, comforting in its tightness. When it came to an end, it happened so abruptly that Tera curled into the smallest ball possible, hiding and frightened.

A voice, that Tera had come to identify as her

mother's doctor, said, "There's a problem with the baby."

And everything changed.

The steady beat of her mother's heart began hammering in her ears, and the sound of blood began to rush around her, louder and louder until it threatened to drown all other sounds out. The walls of her mother's abdomen squeezed inward and Tera felt her environment shrinking.

Her mother's voice, "What . . . what kind of problem?"

Another new sensation entered Tera's awareness. Fear. Her mother was afraid and Tera was afraid. Was the doctor voice afraid? Tera didn't think so.

The doctor voice was speaking again and Tera stretched her awareness out as hard as she could, to hear over the rushing blood and pounding heartbeat that surrounded her. "We got back the results of the triple serum test. There's a good chance that the baby is . . . deformed."

Her mother's body was shaking. What did "deformed" mean?

"A chance?" her mother said.

"A very good chance. Obviously, we'll want to perform an amniocentesis to confirm it, but the test is usually very accurate."

"How . . . how bad?" Her mother's voice had changed, was lower then it had been before.

"It varies quite a bit," said the doctor voice. "Typically, we see a very high rate of Down's Syndrome, which can include heart defects, mental retardation, and more obvious physical signs such as an abnormal tongue, eyelids, or hands." The doctor voiced paused, then continued. "It's also possible that the fetus will spontaneously abort. Depending on the level of deformity, that happens fairly often when there's physical defects."

"What can I do?" her mother's voice asked.

"Many women in your position choose to abort the pregnancy rather than face the hardships of raising a child with Down's or other medical problems, or deal with a miscarriage further along into the pregnancy."

"Abortion? You want me to abort my baby?"

What did abortion mean, Tera wondered. Was it anything like quitting?

"Mrs. Fossen," the doctor voice said, "I didn't say that. I'm only telling you what some women choose to do. In your case, there's even more to consider."

"What do you mean?" her mother asked, and Tera noticed that her voice was higher than it had ever been before, and there was a warbling quality to it that made it sound uneven.

"It was a real struggle for you to get pregnant. Given the physical problems you've had, your age, as well as the likelihood of fetal deformities, it's possible that having this child could injure or even kill you. Your body may not be able to handle giving birth to an . . . infant like this."

A shudder ran through her mother's body, and Tera curled up tighter. "I've got to talk to my husband," she said.

"I understand," the doctor voice said. "I'm sorry."

Tera felt her mother begin moving, leaving the doctor voice that had said things which upset her. Tera curled tighter, hoping that the calm happiness of her environment would soon be restored.

The conversations that occurred between her mother and her father made things worse — especially after a terrifying ordeal during which a long, sharp object actually entered her environment — but Tera began to get a clearer sense of what the problem with the baby was. She was the baby and the problem.

"Damn it, Katie," her father's voice yelled, "it'll be a . . . a fucking monster for all we know."

"How can you say that?" her mother asked. "It's us, our baby. They're not a hundred percent sure."

"You work in the radiology unit of St. John's and you can ask me that?" he said. "We knew this was possible."

"But . . ." her mother said. "I love her."

"It," her father said firmly. "Think of it as an it."

"It," her mother said, her voice dull and flat sounding.

"I . . . can't lose you, too, Katie," her father said. "It's too much of a risk."

That was the part of all this that bothered Tera. Her mother was obviously in some kind of danger and it was *her* fault. She was hurting her mother. Tera didn't know what a "monster" was, or what "deformed" meant, but it had been obvious ever since the day the doctor's voice had spoken of a problem that her mother was in terrible pain.

"The doctor said it could kill you, Katie," her father was saying. "You could *die* if you don't abort. Is that what you want, for Christ's sake?"

"No," her mother said, her voice so soft that Tera could barely hear her. "But, it's just so hard, David. Maybe I'll miscarry."

"That's not a chance we can take," her father said. "But I know how hard this is for you."

"You don't, damn you," her mother said. "She hasn't been growing inside *you.*"

Tera felt her mother move, begin to cry, and then could sense that her father was very near. She could hear his heartbeat, too. Steady and strong like her mother's had been before all this started. Now, her mother's heartbeat raced and pounded, fluttering in her ears. Had *she* caused that, too?

Tera wasn't sure. She only knew that she loved her mother, loved her father because he loved her mother. They were scared. Tera didn't know what "kill" or "die" meant, but it must be horrible, even more dire than what she had already experienced with the sharp thing and her environment being constricted.

Tera knew she didn't want her mother to be afraid, to die — whatever that meant — but she didn't know how to help her. She thought about it for a long time, floating in her environment, kicking her legs and moving her arms, knowing she was safe.

All it once it came to her. If *she* was the danger to her mother, and she was *inside* her mother, perhaps the best thing would be to leave the environment. Then, her mother would be safe. If Tera was a monster, then maybe when she wasn't inside she wouldn't be a monster anymore. The only problem was Tera didn't know how to leave the environment, and worse, she was scared to leave the environment.

Inside, sounds other than those that came from her mother, were muted. The inside was safe and warm, or at least it had been. The inside was comfortable, if a bit cramped. Still, Tera knew that she had to help her mother. Tera didn't want to be a monster, didn't want to hurt her mother.

With her fingers, she explored the environment again. It was still shaking a little with her mother's sobbing. The environment was smooth under her touch, flexible and soft. Tera could hear her father's voice, "Shhh . . . honey, it will be all right. I know it will."

Her fingers suddenly encountered something different. It was smooth, too, but it didn't seem to come from around her . . . it came from her! Tera explored it as best she could. The object came from her and lead away from the environment. This must be the way out, she thought.

She stretched as far as she could, but remained in the environment. She was scared, but excited, too. She grasped the object tightly, pulling it toward her, as hard as she could. Tera didn't want to be a monster inside her mother. She wanted to see her mother, touch her, smell her, hear her voice sing again.

"David," her mother's voice said. "Something's wrong."

"What is it?" her father said.

Tera felt her mother move again, almost running, like she had when the doctor had said all those things that had upset her. Tera kept pulling. She would see her mother, make her mother safe.

"David!" her mother screamed. "David, I'm bleeding!"

Briefly, Tera wondered what "bleeding" meant, then decided it didn't matter. She rested a moment, then grasped the object again and pulled as hard as she could. Suddenly the environment collapsed around her, covering her face, and Tera scrambled to escape.

"Oh my God," said her father's voice. "What can I do?"

Tera heard her mother say, "Nothing. It's over." And even in her panic, managed to pull one more time on the object, feeling it give way.

Tera felt herself moving. The environment was completely gone now and there was a rushing sound in her ears unlike anything she'd heard before. It was scary and dark and *very* uncomfortable. It was hard to move, to . . . what's the word?, she wondered . . . breathe?

Only then was she certain. She was leaving the environment.

I'm not a monster, she thought, as a new environment that was blindingly white surrounded her. She struggled briefly, afraid because she couldn't hear her mother's heartbeat, couldn't hear anything.

But I'm free now, Tera thought. Mother is safe. She could imagine her mother singing, could almost hear the words to the lullaby, "Singing, singing, singing, I'm singing you to sleep; singing you to slumber, gray and deep."

And then her awareness of everything faded into the rushing sounds and her mother's lullaby, and Tera drifted into the brightness, sleeping.

One Tree Hill

"Quos amor verus tenuit, tenebit."
"Those whom true love has held, it will go on holding."
— Seneca

Just before sunset, General Sharia Shaynok knelt at the top of a small hill overlooking the dusty, empty road she and Gavin had just traveled. Marked on her map as One Tree Hill, it acted as a grassy support for a large, ungainly, and extremely old cottonwood tree. The road had no name that Sharia knew of, and for now, it remained empty as it meandered towards the northwest. Sharia knew that the soldiers she and Gavin had been eluding for the past two days would soon be coming down the nameless road. They were like dogs on the trail of a deer, she thought. No matter how they had twisted and turned they had never been far behind. The lead they had now was the best she had been able to manage, and it wasn't much.

Rising from her knees, Sharia rolled up her map and with a last look at the road, went to check on the exhausted horses. A barely audible groan from the base of the tree stopped her in mid-stride. Sharia knelt down, her armor creaking, and took Gavin's hand. She smiled down at him. "Rest awhile longer, friend. We have some time yet before they get here."

Gavin stared up at Sharia with his intense grey eyes, and a cough briefly racked his lungs before he spoke. "Sharia, we don't have time — you have time. I'm played out." His voice had a wet sound to it, and Sharia knew blood was in his lungs from the sword cut he'd taken while they were escaping. "

"Don't be silly. Your wound isn't that bad." Sharia looked over at the horses as she spoke. "In a few minutes, we'll both be riding out of here."

Gavin regarded Sharia with a slight grin that somehow managed to offset the pallor of his face. "Sharia, listen to me. The wound is bad enough. I'm slowing you down." He coughed again, and Sharia pulled a cloth from her belt pouch to wipe away the thin trickle of bright red blood that ran down his dirty chin. "Besides," he said, "not even a healer could help me now. I've torn something inside." He paused, trying not to cough. "Last night, I think, during the ride."

Sharia uncorked her waterskin and held it to his lips. She poured a small amount into his mouth and watched him swallow with a grimace. After taking a sip for herself, Sharia replaced the waterskin on her belt. "Listen, I'm going to go check on the road and the horses and —"

"Sharia, wait!" Gavin tried to sit up and collapsed back onto his cloak which Sharia had used to cover the ground.

"Yes, Gavin, what is it?" Sharia again took his hand.

He said nothing for a moment, just stared up at her as though he were parting the misty past with his eyes. "Sharia, we're a long way from the markets of Soursic. How, in the name of the Gods, did we ever manage to get here? To this place, I mean? It certainly wasn't what we expected." He blinked and shuddered as though cold, although the air was hot and dusty. It was late summer and the plains were browning under the sun.

Not replying, Sharia ran a hand caked with dirt and blood through her short-cropped brown and grey hair. She rocked back on her heels and looked at Gavin. For a moment, she could see him as he was on the day she had bought him in the markets at Soursic — handsome and angry, his black hair shining in the noon sun as if to make a mockery of the barely modest rag he wore. She had never wanted, nor even looked at, the other men offered. Had it not been against all tradition, Sharia knew she would have married him. But that could never happen because he was a slave-companion.

The slave-companions were bred and genetically engineered by the science wizards of Soursic to be many things; advisors, help-meets, sometimes lovers. As a high ranking General, it had been Sharia's right to buy him. She had needed an assistant to help her conquer this land for the Empress, one who could lighten the burdens of interim rulership and advise her on matters both political and military. Gavin could do both. The personal history sheet she'd looked at prior to buying him indicated that Gavin's genes from the maternal line went back through five generations of warriors. He had often sparred with Sharia, demonstrating that he had been well trained with both spear and long sword.

But it was the paternal gene Sharia had found most compelling. His father had once been a tactical advisor to the Empress herself. It was his plan that had placed the Empress in a position of strength unrivaled on the continent. Gavin had been trained to assess situations by his father. That is, with a calculating eye towards success. During their discussions, Sharia found him to be her match in both political and military discussions. He was brilliant, and Sharia considered him her best and wisest investment in the war effort. It was only later on, in the hard light of war, that Sharia began to realize that Gavin was much more than an investment.

Sharia did not have a husband, for so long as she remained an unmarried princess, the possibility of an alliance marriage to one of the other noble houses still existed. Gavin himself would have appreciated this political reality had she talked to him about it. But she had not. Nor had she ever touched him or made even the briefest mention of her growing feelings. First, because she felt that his body must belong to him, regardless of his status as a slave. He wasn't, she thought, property to be used as she wished.

Second, and though it seemed both wasteful and silly now, she hadn't the courage. Sharia laughed to herself. A General, she thought, afraid of rejection by a man! But during this war, Sharia had realized she wanted him, and found herself unable to say a single word about it.

"Sharia?"

"Sorry, I guess I was woolgathering." Sharia saw him smile and wondered how long he had known of her feelings for him. "I will tell you what I think, Gavin, but then we must go. The soldiers will be here soon, and I'd prefer to be gone." She squeezed his hand, and admitted to herself that he was the only thing besides war she had ever really loved. Now it seemed as though she might well lose both. The war was already lost, and Gavin was badly wounded — perhaps dying. She looked down the hill, heard the wind blow across the leaves above her head, watched it make distant dust devils on the road. The sun would be gone within the hour.

"Gavin, you know as well as I how we got here. It happens to even the best generals from time to time.

We made errors in judgment about the people here. We thought they could be conquered one province at a time, with minimal casualties to ourselves. Mostly, we didn't think they would organize a rebellion so quickly, and certainly not at my headquarters!" Sharia shook her head, remembering how her outrider sentries had warned her at the last minute. Falling at her feet, the messenger gasped out her report with her last breath: 'The castle is surrounded, and we're hopelessly outnumbered. Escape if you can!'. Now Sharia sighed. "We just made too many mistakes. I should've known better, should've trusted my instincts. Damn, I'm tired."

Gavin said nothing for a minute, waiting to make sure she was through. "It's not entirely your fault, you know. I, too, thought we could take this land easily. I'm your principal advisor, and a portion of the blame is mine." He paused, looking up at the tree. "It's pretty here."

"Yes, Gavin, my friend, it is. But it's time to go. The soldiers will be here soon, peasant dogs that they are." Sharia rose to get the horses, then stopped and looked down at him. "Gavin, I . . . I want you to know sorry I am about all this. I-"

"Shush, Sharia, I know." He coughed several times, and waited for the spasm to pass. He wiped his lips off, and smiled a red smile. "I know, Sharia." His eyes locked with hers for a moment, then he added quietly, "And that is enough."

Sharia did not hear his last mumbled comment as she turned away. Walking towards the chestnut-colored mare that Gavin had been riding, her thoughts turned to escaping the soldiers and this land. Her Empress would — probably — forgive her failure here, although Sharia would insist that she send another General, someone younger and more bloodthirsty, to re-take what had been lost. This land would be taken, but not, she thought to herself, by me. She was going to retire. Once Gavin was better, she would say to hell with allegiances, alliances, and tradition. She would marry him, and devote her remaining years to more peaceful pursuits. She was, as she had told Gavin, tired. Occupied with her thoughts, mainly how Gavin might not be able to ride, Sharia concentrated on tending to the exhausted mare. She did not see how he was watching her.

Gavin coughed again, several times as he watched Sharia work. He did not, however, let it interfere with his own. In his mind, he was counting the number of hours to the coast and escape. He know the statistics well for travel by horse, even for a tired one. He also knew he was dying — physician skills had been part of his training. Knowing this, and knowing that he was slowing Sharia's escape made his decision easier. He decided, in a way that seemed awfully detached to himself, that admitting his feelings was painful. He knew he loved Sharia, wanted to be with her, although it was unheard of for a General to take a slave-companion as a husband. He also knew that escape, given the numbers and the circumstances, was nearly impossible for them both.

He could not tell her to go. She would see it as quitting, which came hard to her. So he would just do it. To save her, and perhaps it would be enough for him to know that she lived and had loved him in her own way, in what time they had had together. It might even be enough to commend his soul into the next world, where all warriors could feast at the high table.

Reaching a trembling hand down to his right thigh, Gavin stared up at the fading light through the leaves, and unsheathed the dagger Sharia had given to him before starting this doomed campaign. He did not look at it, or at her, fearing that he would lose his nerve. Clenching his sweaty, shaking fist around the dagger hilt, he breathed a final prayer for Sharia's escape and his own soul. As another coughing fit shook his frame, he kissed the tip of the blade with his bloodied lips, raised and reversed it, and drove it with the last of his strength into his own chest. He died with a barely audible groan. In death, Gavin was smiling, his face stained only a little by the tears he had not known he cried.

Sharia turned when she heard Gavin groan and the dull thud of a dagger piercing flesh. The blood drained from her face as she saw the hilt of a dagger protruding from Gavin's still chest. For a moment, she looked around wildly for an unnoticed enemy. One great, horrified inhalation later, Sharia's scream echoed across One Tree Hill and into the barren plains beyond it. She fell onto her knees beside him and gathered him into her arms.

Sharia cried in spite of herself. I am, she reflected as she rocked his cooling body, the conqueror, conquered. After what seemed a long while, Sharia looked back down the road, now barely visible in the last light of day. In the distance, a dustcloud was moving in her direction. It was then that Sharia know what she should do, what she must do. Gavin had been right, she knew that he thought escape impossible.

She laid Gavin's body on the ground underneath the cottonwood tree. She wiped off his dirty, peaceful face, pulled the dagger from his chest with a sob, and gave him the kiss she should have given him before he died. Sharia covered his body with her own cloak, royal emblem over his still heart as though he was nobility. Turning away toward the horses, she stripped the saddle off the mare, then her own mount. Slapping them both on the hindquarters, she sent them trotting down the hill. Some lucky peasant would find them, and perhaps thank the Gods for his fortune. Sharia would not be needing her horse anymore. She was done running.

The first stars became visible in the eastern sky, as Sharia, with a watchful eye on the approaching dust-cloud, pulled her sword from the scabbard and began to polish it. She dusted off her dirty armor as best she could. She knew she would be fighting in near darkness, the only light that of the stars and the red crescent moon that hung low on the horizon. Because she held the higher ground, she would be at a slight advantage. Sharia smiled at the oncoming soldiers, though they couldn't see it yet. She waited, and reflected on how many of them she could kill before she herself died. Untrained as most of them were, she thought, there would be a large harvest for old lady Death tonight.

A short time later, the first of the peasant soldiers saw the gleam of her sword in the dark, a brief reflection of light from their torches. Sharia waited for them. As they approached the hill, Sharia called down to them. "Well, dogs, I see you've finally caught up. So come then! I will kill many of you, perhaps all of you, for this is the price of his death and mine!"

The leader of the soldiers, an ungainly man with a wandering eye, answered her. "Nay, General. Surrender yourself. You're already defeated. Your army is gone, you have no horses, and no escape. We'll be merciful." This last remark was greeted with a few stray chuckles from his men.

"Come up then, dog-leader," Sharia said. "I've a mercy of my own for you. Or are you a coward?"

The leader stared up at the dark figure on the hill. He could hear the few pieces of scavenged armor his men wore creak as they wondered if he would stand being called a coward. He motioned to several of his soldiers. "Go up there and get her. Kill her if you have to."

From the top of the hill, the soldiers could hear Sharia laughing softly. "I'm waiting, oh leader of puppies!"

The three selected soldiers started up the hill while the others watched. The leader said nothing. The first clang of metal on metal rang out earlier than he expected — Sharia had met them partway. The silhouettes were hard to make out, only the sounds of warriors grunting, the clash of swords, and then silence. One figure remained standing in the dark. "Boys," the leader called, "did you get her?"

Suddenly, three heads landed one by one at his feet. "Hardly, peasant. I'm not surprised you sent children to do an adult's job. If this is your best, I'll still be here come sunrise!" Sharia laughed again, a mocking sound.

The leader of the peasant soldiers motioned to the others with him to come closer. In a harsh whisper he said, "That's it, then. We rush her together. She can't take all of us." His voice shook only a little, then he raised his hand high above his head. When he lowered it, he and all thirty-one of his men rushed up the hill with a roar. Sharia watched them come, raised her sword in traditional salute, and did indeed begin to reap a great harvest.

She killed the leader first, her dagger finding the white blob of his wandering eye easily in the dark. The leader, whom Sharia did not even have a name for, fell with a scream. Three others died before Sharia had been injured at all. She killed a fifth peasant at the same time as she took a slice on her left arm, leaving it dangling uselessly at her side. Two more died nearly as easily, but Sharia knew she was starting to slow. She had lost a lot of blood now, and was surrounded. They seemed to be striking from all sides at once, the way dogs will do when they've cornered the deer. Sharia's breath came in quick gasps. "Come on, you mongrels. Come on, you little boys. Is this the best you can do?" She smiled in the darkness. Her once strong voice bubbled weakly in her lungs.

The peasants fell on her with a final roar, and General Sharia Shaynok died without making a sound. The wind blew, and the peasants waited for sunrise to bury the dead. When they found her body, not one word was said.

Some three years later, underneath a fully blossomed cottonwood tree, a young girl found a dagger on One Tree Hill. It was encrusted with old blood and dirt, half-buried beneath a pile of weeds. She did not know the story of General Sharia Shaynok, nor had he heard of Gavin, the slave-companion who had died with her. The girl only knew that somehow this place was special. It had a mark of peace on it. And so she went there to watch the sunset over the road while cottonwood blossoms flew through the air like summer snow. She polished her dagger, letting the light catch on the still-bright blade, and dreamed of one day being a princess and a warrior.

Omega Time

1.
Auto Launch, 25 Minutes

"All that matters is that we're together. *Together.* The where, the how, even the why of it is unimportant. All that matters is that we can see and touch each other, love each other, *be* together. That's all that matters.'"

I can remember her saying this to me late one night in bed, just after we were married. It's been too many years, and I can't recall what prompted this statement, nor even the discussion that followed — and I'm sure there was one. Just as I'm sure that we made love that night; the passionate breathtaking kind that happens early in marriage and goes on for hours and hours where more of your time is spent on kissing and giggling than is ever spent in doing the actual deed. That time when you are discovering each other, exploring the lost continents of the body, finding yourself in the other. It was a long time ago.

It was long before what the scientists have dubbed

Omega Time — the end of all things. I know a lot about it — I'm one of the scientists, as was she. Now, though, she is gone, out there among the stars, and I am here, for better or for worse, and watching Omega Time take its inevitable toll on planet Earth. The last ship, my ship, will auto launch in just under a half hour. About two, maybe three hours after that, the sun will finish its rapid growth into a red giant star and the Earth will be ashes on the solar winds.

I don't think I'll miss it all that much.

2.
Auto Launch, 15 Minutes

I miss her. The smell of her skin, lilacs; the way her eyes sparked like angry blue stars when she laughed; the way she whispered, just before sleep, that she loved me, would always be with me. She didn't lie, of course; she just didn't know.

And that sums up Omega Time so well — nobody knew. After all the calculations had been done, what it really amounted to was nothing more than a simple mathematical error, the kind they made back when humans were using desktop computers and hand held calculators, back before the invention of true cybernetics. Hell, I'd had advanced geocalculus and quantum mechanics program chips installed way back in high school.

But then again, even the best program chips can have

flaws. So, the calculation-prediction on when the sun would go red giant had been off by a little, just 5,000 years or so. The human race has advanced so far, changed so much, but we are still babes compared to the stars — not prescient beings of light, but animals made of blood and bone and fear.

Who would think that such frailties could lead to the Omega Time?

By the time we'd caught the error, it was almost too late. A mass exodus from the planet ensued, and my wife, my joy, was among the first to leave — they needed a geneticist with them — and though we promised to meet at the rendezvous station set up safely beyond the hot zone, it was not to be. She never made it to the rendezvous station in orbit around Saturn's moon, Triton — a cold place of barren, icy landforms and liquid hydrocarbon seas, but with a nitrogen rich atmosphere much like Earth. It had been hoped that with the change in the Sun, and some advanced terraforming, Triton might become a permanent way station to the stars.

But her ship had a major oxygen malfunction only 38 minutes after taking off and had exploded into a gigantic ball of fire that quickly went out in the cold vacuum of space. No one lived, of course. No one lived.

Now she's out there, among the stars she loved to look at, but knew so little about, returned to the cosmos, her promises to be with me always so much ash.

But I lived. I had to. I had to go on living and helping, trying to save as many as we could. And most of them, those who hadn't gone into hiding somewhere here on Earth, and those whose hastily constructed ships — like my wife's — hadn't blown up in route to the station — had made it to safety.

3.
Auto Launch, 10 Minutes

My ship is the last one. I am the only one on board, and I am more than qualified to fly it with the help of the computer — my time as both an astronaut and an astrophysicist has seen to that. The final data streams from our growing sun are already set to transmit to the station. But I'm not going to the station. I'm going to the stars, returning myself to the cosmos to keep our mutual promises.

She would have wanted me to do it this way, I think. To have stayed long enough to help as many people as I could, and then to join her.

I remember our wedding night, and — like an old man in physical stasis, whose body has failed but whose mind continues to remain annoyingly sharp — I've gotten sentimental about it. I still celebrate our anniversary, still set out the dishes and the wine goblets that were kept all these years, still drink a toast in our honor. Then, when it's time, I go into our room and lay down upon our empty bed. I ache for her presence, the soft touch of her hand on my cheek, her breath tickling the hairs on the nape of my neck — but these things are like wraiths in my mind. I remember them but they slip away before I can touch them. I lay there remembering how she looked, her skin alabaster in the moonlight from the windows, her eyes flashing. It makes me smile to remember these things.

The last time we made love, the night before she launched into the infinite sky to find not freedom but death, she drew me into our bedroom, pulled me down onto the synth-silk comforter. She didn't want to go, but had to go, much as I had to stay. That night she was fiercely passionate, sometimes crying, sometimes laughing, reminding me of all the reasons that I loved her.

Now on our anniversary I lay in bed and wonder if some part of her, deep in her womb, knew she was already dying. I didn't, only knew that I wanted to be with her, a part of her, that she could take a part of me with her. But technology and love are mutually exclusive — at near-light speed, a flickering heartbeat, a hand raised in desperate farewell, is invisible.

I think of this launch as my arms reaching for her, a supreme gesture of fire and desperate wanting as I head toward the stars where she rests.

4.
Auto Launch, 5 Minutes

The ship is ready to go, and strapped in I can already imagine seeing her again. The flight path is programmed for the heart of the sun, the heart of my life. The journey, waited for so long, will be short — a few minutes as fast as this ship will travel. We will be reunited among the stars and the heat, and perhaps in some other form I can't even begin to grasp, we will speak our vows again. She is out there, waiting for me, our promises to be fulfilled.

5.
Auto Launch, 1 Minute

Over the roar of the igniting engines I can hear her laughter, her voice calling to me. I close my eyes and bring her form into focus. She is smiling. She is stretching out her arms to me, wanting to hold me again, sorry we have been apart for so very long. The ship is very fast. I love her, and there is no other for me in this universe of possibility. I will be with her soon.

I remember a colleague once telling me that women were like stars, they were tricky, bright, and seemingly everywhere at once. I don't know about other women, but he was right when it comes to her. She is here somehow, with me again, already by my side in the cockpit, yet I know that she is Out There, too.

I unbuckle my shoulder straps so I can kneel at her feet. I have missed her so much that to be this close and not touch her is unbearable. Her hands stroke my hair.

6.
Auto Launch

We are together again, the rocking of the ship as it blasts through the atmosphere, making its way toward another place, the gentle rumble of a spring thunder. Her kisses are moist with her tears. She is crying and telling me silently that she has missed me, too. She is sorry. She didn't want to break her promise to be with me always.

7.
Post Auto Launch

I shush her, caress her hair, forgive her as I wrap myself in her warmth. She meets me halfway, and we hold each other like twin stars caught in a gravity well. I can feel her smiling against my shoulder as though being with me is a joy for her.

We move together with the ship. Her arms cling to my back, a hug that stretches on like the cosmos. The sun is blinding and hot, and the pillow of her hair is damp with sweat and tears. It's hard to breath, she's squeezing me so tight, and she looks infused with joy — almost burning with an inner light and heat. Vaguely, I wonder how long we have before the Sun takes us, then dismiss all, focusing on her.

It is almost finished now. The heat in the ship is unbearable and sweat rolls of our bodies and pools on the metal deck of the floor only to evaporate in a hiss of steam. Our sounds — crying, laughing, whispering — mingle with the sounds of the ship, the sounds of the hull creaking under the strain as the Sun's gravity takes us.

We're going faster now, the Sun is burning through the metal plates that protect the ship and in the cabin, it's so bright I have to close my eyes. It doesn't matter — I can still see her. The heat reaches an apex, a moment when it passes beyond anything imaginable, and then, all at once, I am cool. A chill passes between us.

We are there, and time slows itself to the film reel of memory. She cries out my name, and I tell her that I love her. That I was wrong — technology and love are not mutually exclusive. This ship has brought me back to her. It is quiet and I can hear the ship burning. I can hear her breath, feel it on the nape of my neck. Her hand, like a wraith, touches my cheek.

We are children in the Sun, our shadows stretching across the burning cosmos, our lives and memories ash, our time passing into the infinite span of sparking stars.

Then, I know four things almost at once.

The ship is at the end of its flight path.

I can smell lilacs on her skin.

We are together.

I love her, even in death, even in Omega Time.

Seven Year Itch

Shauna woke to cool darkness and silence, unable to move her arms because they were tied to something above her head. For a split second, before she was completely awake, she panicked, struggling against her bonds, her back arched into the air and her mouth open in an effort to scream. Then she sagged in relief. Her husband, Gordon, was fulfilling one of her fantasies.

A dark one.

She took stock of her situation. A blindfold covered her eyes, soft and secure, the cloth reminding her of the delicate folds of a butterfly's wing. It must be silk. Her hands were tied – silk, too? – above her head, and very little movement was possible. She was laying on a padded table of some kind. Her legs were also tied, and then she realized something else. She was totally nude.

A whisper of warm air folded over her body and her nipples responded.

"Gordon?" she said.

Her answer was silence, and Shauna felt it then - the dull ache that centered itself in the deepest part of her belly and spread like fire over her clitoris and across her vaginal lips to end, an itch she couldn't scratch, along her inner thighs. She had been married to Gordon for seven years, and she sighed into the stillness of the room, and licked her lips, thinking of him, of what he might be doing.

She heard a sound then – a footstep? – and silence returned.

"Gordon?" she whispered again.

"Shhh," a voice said. It had a harsh, rasping quality to it.

For a long second, Shauna's mind spiraled in the darkness. Did she know that voice? Was it Gordon's voice? And in her mind, her inner voice wailed in the blackness, "... *nooo* ..."

And then she did scream. Long and loud into the silence, while her mind gibbered with fear and wonder and an odd sense of loathing. Where was Gordon? What had happened?

Who was there?

When she hitched her breath, the voice said again, "Shhh." And she heard the sliding sound of footsteps on concrete.

"Who's there?" she cried. "Who are you?"

"Shhh," the voice whispered, the rasp of it sliding over her like a cat's tongue. "I won't hurt you, I promise."

"Get . . . get away from me, you bastard!" she shrieked. "Where's Gordon? Where's my husband, what have you done to him?" She could feel her pulse racing, hear the labored sound of her own breathing, and smell the faint odor of her own cold sweat. Her own fear.

"I'm afraid," the voice said, "that Gordon is unavailable at the moment. But don't worry, he asked . . . no, asked isn't quite the right word . . . he begged me to take good care of you." She felt a finger trace a delicate path along the line of her jaw, and her whole body tensed. "And so I shall," the voice concluded.

"What have you done to him?" she hissed. If I show any more fear, she thought, I'm dead.

"Nothing," the voice said. "Nothing at all. He is, after all, fulfilling *your* fantasy."

"But this wasn't my fantasy!" she said. "Let me out of here, right *now*."

The voice chuckled, and Shauna remembered an alley cat she'd seen once. A big one, with matted gray fur and a huge head. At the time, she'd thought to rescue it perhaps, but when it turned, she saw that it's teeth were exposed, long needlepoint daggers, and from between them, a rat's tail twitching in agony. It's eyes, the golden red of sunset on cornstalk leaves, pinned her for a moment, and it rasped a horrible, burping meow around its meal. This voice reminded her of the cat, and another shudder passed through her.

"It's easy to say that now, Shauna," the voice said. "When you're frightened and alone and the dark is so achingly cold. But Gordon said you were quite specific. You wanted to be blindfolded and tied, pleasured by a stranger in every possible way, never to see his face, never to know who it was. Not quite rape, not quite love, but something . . . darker, something different." The finger traced a path over her erect nipple. "I am the stranger, Shauna."

She screamed again then, and over her own wretched noise, she could hear the stranger laughing. Oh God, why did I ever admit to such a horrible, wretched thing? And her own mind provided the answer, *Because you hungered for something new after seven years of the same old same old. And now you've got it. So much for keeping the lines between fantasy and reality separated.*

And was it possible that the heat and the wetness she'd felt between her legs earlier was still there, was in fact, even more noticeable than before? Nonetheless, she had to stop this. It had been a *fantasy*, nothing more, and while Gordon had joked about fulfilling it for her as he had so many others, it had always been a joke. Hadn't it? She'd thought so, and it was one thing to fantasize about a stranger, and quite another to actually do it. She loved Gordon, had been loyal to him since the day they'd started dating.

"Listen," she said. "I've changed my mind. This isn't what I thought it would be. It's . . . it's cheating and it's scary. Untie me, please."

"Gordon said you would say that," the stranger said. "He told me to ignore you, no matter how you begged to be freed. He said that he was paying me good money to do a service and he wanted a good service for you." The voice chuckled again, and Shauna could imagine the smile.

"No," she said. "I don't want this. I don't want it at all."

"You'll change your mind," the voice said. "I guarantee it." The first touch felt like a feather, and she stiffened, her arms and legs straining against the bonds.

"No," she repeated. "No."

"Yes," the voice said, right in her ear, "Oh, yes." A tongue caressed the delicate flesh of her earlobe, and marked a wet trail down her neck. She didn't want to respond, but her body betrayed her. She felt her breath catch in her throat and her nipples felt like hot pebbles on her breasts.

I can't do this, she thought, I can't. *But you are,* her mind said, and she felt the strangers fingers caress first one nipple and then the other. *And you want to.*

"No, I don't," she said, speaking aloud, startling herself.

"So you've said," the voice replied. "But since Gordon gave it the thumbs up, why not enjoy it?" The feather was back, this time sliding along her spread legs and tickling her inner thigh.

She imagined it was made of ostrich feathers dyed black, and when they reached the outer folds her labia, she gasped, involuntarily arching to meet the sensation. "Because I can't," she said. "I love my husband."

"And he must love you," the stranger said, "to be willing to share your lovely body with anyone." The fingers were moving again, caressing and then pinching her nipples, tracing paths around her clavicles and then returning to her breasts.

"No, that's not how it is," she said.

"Then how is it?" the stranger asked.

Shauna thought about her answer carefully, trying to restrain her breathing, trying not to show how the situation, the feeling of helplessness, the sensation of sweat and darkness, was turning her on. "He doesn't want to share me," she finally said. "He just wants me to be . . . happy. Fulfilled. And this time it's gone too far."

"Happy and fulfilled, is it?" the stranger said, laughing. "Oh my, how delightful."

"Why is it delightful?" she snapped, hating his mockery.

"Because happiness doesn't come from activity, or fantasy, or money. Happiness comes from within. And it's so intensely personal that even this — " and he slipped a strong finger between her wet vaginal lips and she gasped at the sudden penetration - "is nothing."

She didn't answer, was afraid to answer. God how she wanted it, wanted to be ravaged, taken. She *was* happy with Gordon, but the years had made sex more demanding, more challenging as they grew to know what the other wanted. It's easy to be lazy in the bedroom, she thought.

Then his finger was back, and she didn't try to pull away. She couldn't, not anymore. Whatever self-control she might have had was lost in the intensity of the moment, and maybe the stranger was right. Gordon wanted this, too. Had set it up for her, and delivered her here somehow. Had even hired this man to pleasure her.

Shauna could feel her clitoris swelling beneath the gentle probing of the finger, could feel the wetness spreading from between her legs, down her inner thighs. She bit down on her lower lip, hard, and the faint copper taste of blood filled her mouth. She was torn in a way she had never imagined between want and right.

Another finger was added, and almost against her will, she pushed her hips into the pressure. A soft moan escaped her lips. In her mind, the battle between yes and no, want and right, was over. She arched her hips. "It's too much," she said. "Too much."

"I know, Shauna," the stranger said. His breath, his voice in her ear, her mind, while his hands played her body like a cello. Her nipples were so hard it almost hurt, and they burned.

The stranger rubbed his face down her neck, and over her breasts, the stubble of his cheeks a sharpened file against her fevered skin. He leaned against her, and she knew without touching him that he was naked. She felt his hard torso press against her.

His lips found hers, his tongue probing and wet, and she felt him climb onto the table. He straddled her, and Shauna could feel his hardness pulsing against her mound, hungry and insistent. She wanted it, wanted him inside her, and she was ready. The oddity of the situation, the way it had been sprung on her, a dark surprise, the feathers, the touching, her very own helplessness combined into a powerful aphrodisiac that she could not resist.

"Take me," she whispered. "Take me now, right now."

"Not yet," he said, his words spoken into her mouth. He kissed his way down her body, licking her nipples, biting them, and going still lower, over her trimmed pubic thatch, and finding, with remarkable ease, the swollen button of her clitoris. She bucked beneath him, her legs spread as wide as her bindings would let her go.

"Yesss," she said. "Oh, God, that's nice."

His tongue began to lap at her then, and he slipped first one finger, and then a second inside her. He used his other hand to open her lips, and his tongue was a hard wetness against her clit.

"That's it," she said. "Faster."

He moved faster, his fingers thrusting inside her, his tongue bouncing off her engorged clitoris. She tensed, feeling the orgasm begin, and cried out, her hips bucking and twitching against the table. "Oh, God," she screamed, "yes!"

He must have felt her climax, because his fingers went faster still, pounding into her, and at the exact right moment, he bit down - hard! - on her clitoris, and she came again. He continued playing her with his tongue until her moans and contractions stopped, and her breath, hot and fast in the cool air, slowed a little.

Shauna felt him move then, and a twinge of fear returned to her. She had abandoned herself to this man, this stranger. She didn't know him, and Gordon . . . did Gordon know him?

"That was incredible," she said. "Like nothing I've ever experienced."

"It's not over," the cat voice said, "not yet, anyway." His fingers moved up her torso, found her sensitive nipples, pinched them lightly. "You wanted to be ravaged, remember?"

"Yes," she said, "but I . . ."

"No buts," the voice said sternly.

His weight pressed down on her, his tongue finding her lips and licking them. She could feel his hard shaft, insistent, against her thigh. The taste of him, the smell of him was new to her, an illicit thrill as she'd been with no other man than Gordon in seven long years. Blinded, her senses sought to compensate. Her ears heard every breath, every subtle moan, the sliding of skin on skin, and even, it seemed, the drip of sweat from the stranger's brow onto her burning flesh. Her sense of touch was better, too, and each place of pressure, each gesture, sent a shudder through her body. Had she ever been this turned on? Had she ever wanted like this?

But then an image of her husband rose up in her mind. Gordon, with his serious eyes, and black hair. His strong body, firmly muscled from working out. Was it fair to him? To fulfill her own deepest, darkest desires, even when it meant violating their vows?

The stranger was still kissing her, licking her, making her body respond, but Shauna felt suddenly distant from it. Had it already gone too far? Would Gordon forgive her if she actually had intercourse with a stranger?

Would she forgive him, if the tables were turned?

"Stop," she said, her voice coming out a choked whisper. "Stop, please."

"Why?" the stranger mumbled into her shoulder.

"I mean it," she said, "stop right now."

The kissing stopped, and Shauna breathed a sigh of relief. "I can't do this," she said. "I thought I could, and I wanted it, God knows I did, but I can't."

Odd as it was, she would have sworn she heard the

stranger smile. "Why?" he asked.

"Because I just realized that the sex isn't what the fantasies were really about," she said.

"Oh?" the stranger asked, his voice strangely noncommittal. "Then what were they about? Aren't all sexual fantasies about sex, about wanting the things we can't have, our deepest, darkest desires?"

"No," she said. "The best fantasies, my best fantasies, are really about him. About keeping what we have alive and vital, a . . . an urgent kind of heat to keep ourselves interested.

"I don't want you," she said. "I want Gordon."

The stranger said nothing, but he climbed off of her, his feet hitting the concrete with a sharp slapping sound. Shauna felt her bonds being loosened, first her feet, then her arms.

She opened and closed her hands several times, stretching them, then reached up to remove the blindfold. For some reason, it seemed important to see this stranger who had, merely by doing what Gordon had told him to do, made her ache with sexual need as she hadn't in some time.

The blindfold came off, and her eyes blinked several times, adjusting to the light. When they cleared, she saw him.

"Gordon," she said. "It . . . it was you?"

He pulled a small black object off his throat. "Yes," he said, his voice once more his own. "It was me." He held up the object. "It's a voice changer," he said. "You put it on your throat and it changes how the sound comes out. Something about vibrations."

She shook her head. "It was you the whole time?" she asked, not entirely believing her own eyes.

He smiled. "The whole time," he said. "And I'm glad."

"Why?" she asked. "I thought –"

"I was fulfilling your fantasy?" he asked.

She blushed, nodded.

"I was," he said, "but in a way I felt comfortable with. I wanted to see how much of it was fantasy, and how much of it was reality."

He crossed the few steps to her, wrapper her in his arms. "I love you, Shauna," he said, "and I'm glad you couldn't go through with it."

"Me, too," she said. "And I do love you." She let him hold her, and relaxed in his arms.

"I didn't mean to scare you," he said. "I know we have an active fantasy life, role-playing and talking to each other, but it's different when it's real, isn't it?"

"Yes," she said softly. "It was exciting at first, then scary, then very arousing. But in the end, I couldn't do it, not really."

"Why?" he asked.

This time she answered for him. "Because seven years isn't all that long. We have a lot to do to each other, for each other before either one of us should think of seeking satisfaction elsewhere."

"How long do we have, you think?" he asked.

"I don't know," she said, "sixty, maybe seventy years."

He was kissing her then, and it felt more than hot. It felt right.

"That ought to do," he said.

She kissed him back, her hands finding his erect penis and drawing him closer. "I hope so," she said, pulling him onto the table with her. "Think we can keep each other satisfied for that long?"

He slipped inside her with delicious friction, and she arched her hips to meet him. "Maybe," he said. "If we're always willing to try."

"I am," she said. "More than ever."

"Me, too," he said. "Now shut up and kiss me."

She did, and the itch disappeared entirely.

PART TWO
Of Memories

Of Memories

I cannot forget to carry them
like pictures in lockets, my only
family heirlooms. Between heat-lightning
and the Platte River, I am standing
after the storm and wearing a rainbow —
a mask of myself, for myself.
Hiding behind it as though my stories,
my chameleon painted lies,
could offer some truth to life or affect death.
Inward turning, I can
make these moments happen:

When I was four, colors were
a human invention, a type of metal
and glass trickery, anything to
make this world more livable.
I asked my father if he liked life
more when the world was black and white.
He failed to answer —
a television clicked to mute.

Once in late summer I wanted to sit
on a rare sand beach on Lake Superior's north shore.
I wanted to tell tall-tales around a driftwood bonfire,

drink mediocre California wines,
look at rocks in the water,
moss on tree trunks,
people who had run to escape a city or a past.
I didn't have the guts.

The colors of pain are different
afflictions for anyone who feels which
is everyone. I heard of an old man
who saw only grays — he fell in love
for the first time, saw yellows, and
it stopped his heart.
They buried him on a Thursday.

Standing on an August bridge, I am
a perfect Mid-Western, cornfield poet.
I cannot escape memory with
conjured words or visions. Looking
at the source of these permanently boiling
clouds — my mother, my father,
my scrapbook of grassland weather,
I know I am at home, and that
I am never leaving.

The Sleepers

for Denise Sweet

"This is to remember / Our wounded and dead /
This is to remember the names we've given away or
 never received/
This is to love the forgotten"
 — Denise Sweet, Constellations

The streets were clogged with traffic. Others, like themselves, were making a desperate attempt to flee the mobs and the fires ravaging the city. Had he been alone, Darien wouldn't have bothered trying to leave — he felt confident in his ability to care for himself. But Tara and Rayanna had no such abilities. He knew that he would have to get them out of the city. Eventually, the traffic had proven too much, and Darien had left the vehicle, and taken Rayanna and Tara forward on foot. He carried Tara, and a portion of their belongings, while Rayanna followed right behind, carrying the rest. Trekking through the insane streets, Darien urged Rayanna to move faster. It was no use however, and soon, she was nearly ten steps behind them. For Tara's sake, Darien felt compelled to keep moving as fast as possible.

When the rioting mob swept out of the alley beside them, Darien had been faced with the awful decision to choose between saving Tara or saving Rayanna. He had tried to do both. The ugly crowd slammed into the streets, increasing the distance between them. Darien ran forward, moving out of the way of most of them, and holding the crying Tara in his arms. He kept moving, holding the Glock in his right hand, and Tara in his left. The heat was oppressive, and Tara clung to him with ferocious tenacity. In reality, it only took him a few minutes to find a place to hide Tara so he could return for his wife.

An empty alley, and no one watching or following. Darien opened the lid of a large dumpster filled with paper, and tossed their belongings inside it.

"Tara," he said.

She was crying into his shoulder, frightened. "What is it, Daddy? Where's Mommy?"

"It's just that crowd, sweetheart. But I need you to be brave for me, ok?"

"Why, Daddy, why? I don't want to be brave. I want Mommy."

Knowing the clock was ticking, that it was probably too late, Darien grasped Tara firmly by the shoulders, and shook her. "Tara, I know you don't want to be brave right now, and I know you want Mommy. I want her, too. You understand that, right?" he asked.

"Yes," she said. She had recently lost her front teeth, and her voice had a lisping quality to it.

"All right, then. Daddy has to go get Mommy because that crowd separated us. I need you to stay here," he pointed, indicating the dumpster. "And I need you to be brave and quiet."

"In there?" she asked. "It'll be dark and smelly."

"I know," Darien said. "But it will be safe until I get back."

"I'm scared, Daddy," Tara said. In the distance, the sound of sirens, screams, and gunshots collided with breaking glass and the roar — somewhere nearby — of a burning building.

Darien shook his head. "It's ok to be scared, honey. Daddy's scared, too. But if — " he paused, about to say he had to go if he was going to save her, "but I really need to go get Mommy, ok?"

Tara nodded, once. "Daddy, is this like when you were in the war? Were you scared then, too?"

"Well, it's kind of like the war. And, yes, I was plenty scared then, too. But you know what?" he asked.

"What?" she said.

"Everything will be fine. I'll be back in five, maybe ten minutes, and then we'll make like bananas and split. O.k.?" he asked, hopeful that this lame joke would do the trick.

"Ten minutes?" she asked.

"At most," he said.

"O.k.," she said. "I'll try to be brave."

Darien lifted her up, and put her in the dumpster. "Tara, I want you to sit down and cover yourself with all that paper. I want you to be really quiet, and wait here for Daddy and Mommy. Can you do all that for me?"

"Yes, Daddy," she said, sitting and beginning to cover herself up. "I'll be super quiet."

Darien blew her a kiss and began to lower the lid. "I love you, sweetheart, and Daddy will be right back."

"I love you, Daddy. You'll bring Mommy?" she asked, her face already shadowed by the lid.

"I promise," Darien said. "Now stay quiet."

She shook her head in the affirmative, and Darien

lowered the lid gently. Then turned and sprinted back out of the alley. He ran much like he had run through the Central American jungles during the war. That had been hell, and he'd always assumed it was the worst thing he could or would ever go through. He'd been wrong. This was far worse than tracking through the mountains and the jungles.

As he moved quickly through the streets, he thought to himself that the Central American War, as it had come to be called, had been a vacation compared to leaving his daughter in a trash bin and hunting through crazed crowds of citizens for his wife. Rounding the last corner, he saw a large group of young men, dressed raggedly, and gathered in a semi-circle. Gaps between the moving circling men allowed him to see a flash of Rayanna's leg. He pulled the Glock from the shoulder holster as he ran, screaming her name, towards the group.

They split apart and Darien fully saw her. Her eyes gazed up at him in mute agony and horror. Her hair was matted with blood; her shirt torn open and her jeans ripped off. On top of her, a young Mexican was thrusting into her body. Darien saw this in a frozen moment, saw that several of them even had their zippers undone, as though they were preparing for their turn, or — God forbid — had already finished. His mind blanked, but his body continued to function as it had been trained.

She was dead — must be dead — and beyond pain or caring. Darien shot the Mexican in the back of the head, the force of the glazer round literally forcing him off Rayanna in a bloody heap. He moved his arm slightly to the right, and the red dot of the internal laser sight illuminated the acne on the next man's forehead. Darien shot him, and he flew backwards, knocking several more down in a pile and covering them with bits of brain and blood.

The remainder of the group split into two directions. Some ran off, heading for safer sport. Four remained and saw Darien grinning like some mad specter from hell. One picked up a large chunk of asphalt and threw it at him. Darien jerked his arm, but the rock hit the barrel of the Glock, knocking it out of his hand.

Darien was breathing heavily; his six-foot, four-inch frame was covered with sweat. He grinned again and opened his arms wide as he moved in.

The first one held a knife out menacingly. Darien circled, making certain that he would face them only one at a time. The knife flashed out, and Darien stepped sideways, caught his attacker's arm and twisted it. He slammed his elbow across the back of the arm, shattering the bone. The man screamed, his head thrown back and the cords standing out on his neck. Spinning, Darien thrust his fist into his throat, crushing his larynx. The man fell, gurgling in his own blood.

The second and third attackers moved in at one time, both wielding crude billy clubs, apparently made from the legs of a kitchen table. Darien mentally gauged his attackers. The one on his right hesitated briefly, and Darien noted that he was favoring his left leg a small amount. He assumed the weakness, stepped towards him, and threw a snap kick into the left kneecap. There was a brief crunching sound, and Darien, remembering the black t-shirted youth behind him, dropped into a crouch. The makeshift club whistled over his head and thudded with bone crunching force into the face of the screaming man whose knee he'd just broken. He went down, crippled.

Darien rose from his crouch, drawing the slim boot knife. He thrust upwards, angling the blade slightly between the third and forth rib, and driving it into the heart. As he lifted, he felt the warm blood rush over his hands, and a moment of disgust came over him. He shoved the dead man, really nothing more than a boy, off the knife and away from him. The last of his assailants looked on.

Darien sagged, putting away the knife. He stared hard at the boy for a moment, then said, "Get out of here. Get out, you son-of-a-bitch, before I kill you, too." The boy fled. Darien turned to the groaning man lying at his feet.

His face was crushed, the nose and cheekbones shattered and broken. Shrugging, Darien pulled the Glock again and shot him in the forehead. It was the only mercy he could offer the nameless boy who might lie there, dying, for hours. He then forced himself to look at his ravaged wife. She was unmoving.

Darien knew that his time was extremely limited. He picked her up and carried her out of the street, lowering her to the sidewalk. With as much care as possible, he removed her jewelry for Tara, and brushed back her matted hair. Then, he straightened her clothes as best he could, and covered her with his field jacket. There was little more he could do. Tara was still waiting, and the crowds could return at any minute. Darien didn't know how to cry anymore, hadn't in years, and this wasn't the time or place for grief. He kissed his wife for the last time, and mumbled a small prayer over her body. "May all of heavens host embrace you as you sleep, may all your wounds be healed, and your name never forgotten. I love you," he said.

Then he turned and went to get Tara. Together, they fled the city . . .

*Darien Blake awoke suddenly, his senses alert to his environment even when he was asleep. The dream again, he thought to himself. Three years ago, his wife had been killed in the mass Chicago riots. Thousands had died as the gangs, the homeless, the drug lords, and (so it seemed) just about anyone who was bored, had gone on a rampage that had all but destroyed the city. Food shortages, water problems, severe poverty — all of these and more had been the spark that had lit the bomb. Darien and his wife, Rayanna, and Tara his nine-year-old daughter had tried to flee the city. All of which has made for one hell of a nightmare, he thought. It'll probably never go away completely.

The dark room was cool, though it was only early autumn. Outside, the drizzling rain had stopped, and Darien could hear the rising wind that caused the branches of the apple and cherry trees in the orchard to creak and sway. Though the wind coming in through the slightly open window was not what had caused him to awaken. Darien was patient, letting his heightened senses sort out the stimuli, looking for something that didn't quite fit. Just the dream again, he thought to himself. It's not the first time it's woken me from a sound sleep. Darien carefully stretched his back and legs, not moving out of the rocking chair next where he'd fallen asleep.

Next to him in her twin bed, his daughter Tara wheezed quietly as she slept. She had been fighting a lung virus — one of the new drug resistant strains — for the past three weeks. Four days ago it had worsened into pneumonia. The doctor had prescribed strict bed rest, and a bag full of drugs. Still, her sleep had been troubled, and Darien was thankful that she was finally resting comfortably. He stood, covered Tara with the blankets she had kicked off in her sleep, and turned towards the door.

As he placed his hand on the doorknob, Darien turned back to the room, thinking he should shut the window. This long-time habit of securing a room before he left it, of double-checking, was what saved his life. Looking through the window, Darien saw a tiny dot of red light that appeared over Tara's bed. He froze for a moment, as the light seemed to race across the lightly painted wall towards him. Recognizing that the dot was, Darien leapt out the door just as the shooter fired. The bullet passed through the screen of Tara's window, buzzed over Darien's shoulder and buried itself in the thick cushions of the couch. There was no report from the shot, and Darien realized that the sniper had a silencer on his weapon. And that meant . . .

That means he's a professional, Darien thought to himself. He was lying prone on the floor, and he stayed that way for several seconds, hoping the shooter wouldn't fire again until he could move out of the house. So long as he was inside, Tara was in danger.

When there was no immediate second shot, Darien decided to move to his room and retrieve his weapons. He low-crawled across the living room floor and into the short hallway that led to his bedroom. Reaching it, he slid across the hardwood floor, and braced his back against the dresser and his legs against the doorframe. He pushed, and the dresser slid towards the other wall, revealing a fairly large trapdoor in the floor. It lifted easily, and beneath it was another panel, this one metal and glowing a soft green from the lighted keypad in its face. Quickly Darien punched in his access code, and the locking mechanism unlatched. He opened the door and began removing items from locker. He knew what each was by feel, though there was some light from the keypad.

The first item he removed was his large frame Glock 9mm. He had used this
weapon so often that it was almost an extension of

his arm. This particular model was state-of-the-art, or had been when he'd first purchased it over ten years ago. Now, he reflected, it was probably an antique. Still, it would serve its purpose.

He holstered the Glock under his shoulder and slid an extra magazine for it under his belt. He slid his boot knife into its sheath, and then, remembering the need for silence, removed a silencer from the floor safe and attached it to the Glock. He looked at the case holding his rifle and decided against it. He didn't have a silencer for it anymore, and it was too bulky for what he had in mind.

Darien stood quickly and crossed the bedroom to the window. Parting the drawn shades slightly, he stared out into the darkness of the orchard, looking for the sniper. The shot had come from this direction and it was the best cover spot. Had their positions been reversed, Darien would have chosen that location himself. While he watched, Darien realized with some amusement, that a part of him had been waiting for this for quite awhile. He felt no fear for himself, but knew that he had to act quickly to protect Tara and to keep her illness from getting any worse.

When the Central American War had ended in 2006, Darien had desperately sought employment to support his family. Eventually, he found that the only work he excelled at was killing people. So he hired himself out as a highly paid assassin. He only worked two or three times a year on particularly delicate projects. His last mission had been just before Rayanna's death. A military dictator in Brazil had needed a permanent vacation. Darien provided it. The money from that and other jobs was enough for Tara and he to live comfortably in their new home.

A small farm house just outside Sturgeon Bay, Wisconsin. It was a safe area, and there was no crime to speak of. No one knew him here, and he and Tara basically kept to themselves. He worked in a small craft shop during the time that she was in school. Still, he had always known that every hunter eventually becomes the hunted. Utilizing an anonymous Internet identity, he had contacted his previous employers and told them he was no longer for hire. He suspected then, and it was confirmed now, that they'd find him sooner or later. They'd want to silence him for good.

A momentary flash of red light in the trees drew his attention. "Ah, ha," he murmured to himself. "There you are." He re-crossed the room, grabbed his black field jacket, and found himself smiling in anticipation. It felt good to be in action again. It was something he'd enjoyed, but had willingly given up to ensure Tara's safety and her future.

As he reached the open area of the living room, he lowered himself to the floor, then began to crawl his way across the carpet. He paused by Tara's door and again listened to her steady breathing. He wished, now more than ever, that Rayanna had lived. Tara needed a mother, and Darien knew he was a poor substitute. Perhaps, one day, he'd meet someone again, though it seemed unlikely to him. Trust, especially for someone in his line of work, was a difficult thing and not something he granted lightly or often.

He moved to the front door and quietly cracked it open. The front porch was dark, and the wind blew early fallen leaves across the driveway. Darien waited, watching for signs of movement. Seeing none, he stepped lightly onto the porch and locked the door behind him.

Silver clouds tracked their way across the sky in the

brisk wind. The moonlight, fractured by the changing sky, alternately illuminated and darkened the trees of the orchard. From his vantage behind a low hedge on the side of the house, Darien knelt and watched again for a sign of his target. He remained perfectly still, occasionally tightening and then relaxing his muscles to avoid cramping. From his earliest training days as part of an elite Army Rangers company, Darien had prided himself on his commitment to physical excellence. The Rangers had changed in the late 1990's, recruiting people such as himself who were physically intimidating, mentally sharp, and technologically literate. An assassin for the new millennium, able to hunt or kill almost any way imaginable. He was close to forty years old, but was in better shape than most men half his age.

His excellence as a killing machine didn't mean, however, that he lacked emotion. He loved Tara more than anything, and would stop at nothing to protect her. His trainers had been able to maintain the delicate balance between the need to be human and the need to fight effectively.

There was another tiny flash of light from the orchards, and Darien marked it in his mental map. There was a large amount of open ground between him and the sniper, but Darien judged that if he ran at a right angle to him, he could reach the trees. Once there, he could circle around the backside of the orchard and come upon the assassin from behind. He shrugged thoughtfully to himself. One way was as good as the other given that the clearing extended around the entire house.

Darien leaped up from his hiding place and ran for the trees. The distance was almost 40 yards. Glancing left as he ran Darien saw the red light marking his progress and he began to zigzag. The first shot kicked up dirt and leaves behind him, and Darien put on an extra burst of speed. It was almost enough.

Diving forward to cover the last few yards, Darien felt the second shot strike him in the left leg, forcing him into a tumbling spin that landed him sideways against a tree trunk. He shook his head to clear it and crab crawled around the backside of the tree and into the shadows. He could feel blood running down his pants leg, and a deep burning sensation where the bullet had plowed through the meaty part of his calf.

He pulled his leg up to examine the wound, and bit back a groan of pain. No point in giving myself away completely, he thought. Lifting his pant leg, Darien found a clean entrance and exit hole. The damage could have been worse, but this would slow him and make him weaker. He pulled off his boot and the blood soaked sock beneath it.

Darien stripped off his field jacket, removed the T-shirt he was wearing underneath, and put his coat back on. Taking out his knife, Darien cut the shirt into long strips and used them to plug the wound and to tie it off. He forced himself to put the bloodied sock back on. It wasn't comfortable, but at the least it would allow him to wear the boot. Standing, he returned the knife to its sheath, and tested his weight on the leg.

A hiss of pain came to his lips, but he held it back. The leg would hold, but if he had to run, he could be in trouble.

He turned and made his way further into the trees, keeping a close watch on the last place he had seen the sniper. The wind picked up a little more speed, and Darien was thankful. It would hide any noise he was making. Given his condition, that would be an issue if the wind weren't already blowing leaves all over the orchard. He stopped again, and watched carefully, expecting the assassin to have moved since he last fired.

"Where are you, you son-of-a-bitch?" he asked softly. "I know you're out there somewhere." Another five minutes went by, and Darien decided to keep moving. He knew about where the assassin had been a few minutes before, and chances were good that he'd still be close by.

He began the long trek around the backside of the orchard. His limp was more pronounced now as the muscle began to stiffen. The bleeding had slowed some, but hadn't stopped entirely. Darien could feel the blood soaking through his makeshift bandages. The burning sensation deepened where the bullet had hit, and he bit his lips against the pain. Despite his injury, he made good time.

Darien leaned against a tree to take stock of his situation. He still felt excited by the action, but the wound changed the situation — he would have to finish his opponent quickly. He drew the Glock and began threading the trees, stopping every few feet to look carefully through the waving branches.

It occurred to Darien that he was curious about the assassin. Who would they have sent to kill him? Pausing under the branches of an apple tree, Darien thought they'd be disappointed. The assassin had made three serious mistakes in attempting to take him out. First, he'd allowed himself to be seen. He should've come closer or adjusted for the reflections of the scope. Second, he should have moved immediately after he fired — that he hadn't, indicated a real lack of knowledge on his part either about his target, or within his profession. And third, Darien thought to himself, was that he missed me.

Looking ahead, Darien saw a shadow form crouched at the base of a tree. He calculated the assassin's position and realized that he had moved, but only ten feet or so. Darien was now ten, maybe fifteen yards away.

He could see the barrel of the rifle pointed outwards over the left shoulder of the assassin. Moving cautiously, Darien began to close the gap, the Glock held in front of him.

At about twenty feet, Darien stopped. He had only to shoot, and the threat would be gone. Tara would be safe. Nobody would come looking for the assassin, though others would surely come. Either way, he and Tara would now have to move now. He began to creep forward, his boots making almost no sound on the carpet of wet leaves and grass. The wind blew, and Darien felt confident that the assassin didn't know he was behind him.

He was now only ten feet away. The assassin hadn't moved much other than to sway slightly, as though he were sitting on his heels. Darien aimed the Glock carefully. It was the first time he had actively sought to kill someone since Rayanna had died. The wind shifted and Darien saw the assassin move with it. The red dot from the laser sight built into the slide mechanism followed the movement steadily. His concentration never wavered as he slowly squeezed the trigger.

The assassin dropped on his back with a dull thud, chopping the Glock from his hand. Darien grunted and rolled, shocked that he had fallen for such a simple trick. His momentum pushed him into the "dummy" assassin, which was nothing more than a few pieces of dark clothing with sticks used to prop it all up. He cursed under his breath as he turned to face his assailant, and got to his feet. His leg briefly threatened to buckle beneath him, but held. He drew the knife from his boot sheath and waited for the black-clad assassin to make the first move.

Strangely, a moment passed while they studied each other, neither moving, as though somehow they were old friends who hadn't seen or spoken to each other in long years. Darien couldn't make out his face. He was wearing a hood, and stood deeply in the shadows of the trees.

He moved to his left, gauging his enemy, who also circled, turning lightly on his feet.

Darien spoke first, still moving, weaving the knife in slow, defensive patterns, and trying to ignore the pain in his leg. "Why didn't you just shoot me?" he asked.

The assassin didn't answer at first. To Darien's surprise, he gingerly removed his own handgun and dropped it on the ground. Then, he also took out a slim boot knife and held it casually in his left hand. His voice was soft against the darkness and the wind, almost emotionless. "I thought I could just kill you and finish my business here. But I couldn't. When I missed, I realized that shooting you at a distance wouldn't satisfy me. We're on equal terms now," he said. "If I can't beat you on equal terms, then I don't want to."

Darien nodded, appreciating this attitude. It was one he shared in many ways, though he wasn't above using any means necessary to get the job done. But between equals, this was the best way. "So be it," he replied. "I've been waiting for this for a long time. How much am I worth?"

"They didn't pay me a thing," the assassin said, then lunged forward with the blade.

Darien skipped aside, avoiding the thrust. "I never worked free," he said. "Why do you?"

The assassin lunged again, this time missing Darien's ribs by millimeters. "Because I wanted you dead in the worst way. You're a deserter."

Darien's jaw dropped in shock. The idea he had deserted anybody was ludicrous.

"What the hell are you talking about?" he asked. "I've

never deserted anyone in my life."

The assassin stepped back and in a smooth underhand motion, brought out a second blade. "Me, you senseless bastard. You deserted me." Then the assassin moved into a moonlit area beneath the tree and removed his hood.

In an instant, Darien's blood ran cold, and his flesh prickled in shock. The assassin was Rayanna. "How?" he gasped, trying desperately to understand, to make his numb senses work.

"You left me there to die," she answered. "And I did for all the good it did me. But the medics who found me managed to get my heart started again. I spent three weeks in a coma and almost a year in the hospital recovering. I've spent the last two years training myself and looking for you."

Darien stared at his lost wife. "I didn't know. How could I know?" he asked. "I killed the bastards who attacked you. But I had Tara to worry about. You know it was crazy there. The streets were filled with every kind of loony there is. I had to get her to safety." He held out his hands. "Please, Ray, I don't want to fight you."

She held her knife at the ready. "Tara," she scoffed. "Don't even speak her name to me. When this is over, she's as dead as you are. She's yours now and you're both traitors."

"You'd harm Tara?" he asked, stunned.

Rayanna ignored the question. "I knew I'd find you eventually, and I did. When did you start using my mother's maiden name to work under?"

Darien's mind was racing. If only he could get the knife away from her, then maybe he'd somehow be able to talk sense into her. She was obviously delusional. "As soon as we got here," he said, then slowly began to move toward her. "I can't let you hurt Tara, Ray. I won't. And I don't think you're good enough to kill me."

Rayanna moved backwards, keeping the distance between them. "I will kill you," she said. "Then I win the game."

"Is that what this is to you?" he retorted. "A game?"

"That's what you used to call it," she said. "In your sleep."

"And so you knew the whole time?" he asked.

She nodded. "Of course I knew," she said. "But I didn't care. It paid the bills and allowed us to be a family. Then you betrayed me." She moved forward to meet him, drawing a second blade from her belt. "You destroyed all that, Darien. And now, I'm going to destroy you!"

As she lunged, Darien tried to skip out of the way. He didn't want to hurt her, only to disarm her. Running through his mind was all the unspoken hopes of the last three years. They could be a family again. Tara could have a mother again. Life would begin again. As he moved, the leg finally decided to rebel, and collapsed under him. Her left hand missed, slicing air over his head. But she caught him with the right, slicing him open in a six-inch gash. He clutched at it as he fell.

"Damn," he murmured. He backpedaled as quick as he could, trying to buy time. He watched as she came toward him again, knives raised. Overhead, the last of the rain clouds drifted off, and for a second her eyes were illuminated as they stared down at him.

Those green eyes that had stared at him in love and death were now filled with hate. There was no love left for him in that stare. The dead do not love, he realized, and it is a pointless waste of time to love them as more than a memory. Suddenly, as though a blanket had been torn from around his head, Darien saw what his life during the last three years had become. A dream —

a long sleeping dream from which he had just now awoken. His wife, his real wife and Tara's mother, was dead. Three years ago on the wild streets of a dying city. This woman, this thing, was nothing more than a hate-filled machine whose delusions, much like his mental and emotional sleep, had sustained her through three dark years.

Rayanna leaped at him, trying to finish him quickly. He rolled left and brought his right boot up to meet her charge, driving the air from her stomach. She fell heavily, and her knives fell flew from her hands as she hit the ground. Darien kept rolling, grabbing up his dropped handgun. Using a tree, he levered himself to his feet. Finding the barrel clear of debris, he pointed it at her.

She stood and turned to face him. "You won't do it, Darien," she said, with a grim smile. "You didn't have the guts to take care of me three years ago, and you don't have the guts now. Besides, I don't think you'd rob Tara of her long-lost mother. A girl needs her mother, don't you think?" she asked, moving towards him.

"Yes I do," he said, sighing, "but not you." He pulled the trigger.

*D*arien walked with his daughter through the apple and cherry blossoms that fell like giant snowflakes in the late spring wind. Reaching the very center of the orchard, they sat on a bench and held hands. Neither said much, though occasionally they would talk softly.

Not far from the bench, a memorial stone held both their attentions. It had been erected not long after the early thaw, a tribute to Rayanna as a wife and mother. Tara looked up to see her father staring at the stone, some strange emotion playing across his face.

"What are you thinking about, Daddy?" she said.

Darien said nothing for a moment, then, "Well, I was thinking about your mother and how much she meant to us both."

Tara smiled knowingly. "And?" she asked.

"What do you mean 'and'?" Darien said.

"I know when you don't say everything that's on your mind," she added.

"To tell you the truth, Tara, I was thinking about asking you a question. And it kinda has to do with your mother in some ways I guess."

Tara grinned up at him. "You want to ask LeAnn from the store on a date, don't you?" she said.

Darien turned to her, surprise written on his face. "How'd you know?" he asked.

"Jeez, Dad, you'd have to be asleep not to notice the way you look at her," she said, laughing.

Darien laughed with her. "Yeah, I guess maybe you're right." He looked at her closely, seeing the green eyes so much like Rayanna's, and so full of life. "What do you think?" he asked.

She took his hand again. "I think it's a great idea," she said, gesturing to the memorial stone. "And I think Mom would approve, too."

"I guess maybe she would," Darien said. "I guess maybe she would."

Together, they stood and returned through the trees, leaving the memorial stone to its long, dreamless sleep under the branches.

A Kiss of Fire

*T*he flames were orange and yellow tongues of light and heat eating away at the last remnants of the building. In fifteen years of fighting fires, James had never imagined a building could burn so fast. Through his boots and his heavy clothing, he could feel the superheated air. Beneath him, the groan of the structural timbers as the building struggled against its own weight, was like a distant whale song. Somewhere below, a window burst with an odd shatter-pop sound and sparks danced up toward the cold heavens.

He knew his mind was playing tricks on him — time had ceased to have meaning and his senses focused on small details. His brain knew he was dying, though he still breathed, his heart beat on in a steady, if somewhat accelerated rhythm.

James realized that he couldn't hear the sirens from the fleet of emergency vehicles, but somehow, over the hungry roar of the flames, he could hear the water from the hoses, gushing upwards in a fruitless effort to save the building, save him perhaps, then falling back to earth, frozen droplets of ice. It was cold out, damn cold, and his breath, even standing on top of the inferno, left his body in great gusts of white, like little bits of his soul escaping with each passing breath.

"James? James, hang in there. We're going to get you down."

The voice was muted and crackled, coming at him from a thousand miles away.

"James? James?!" the voice called.

He remembered his radio, pulled it from beneath his coat, as the voice of Captain Mertz continued calling to him. He ignored it, knowing that to answer was to force them to continue trying to save him. There would be no saving him — the building was burning horrendously fast, the water doing little to slow it down. Unbidden, his memory brought forth the image of himself as a six year old boy playing with matches in a field across from his parent's house. And how quickly the summer grass had caught and burned. He shook his head to clear the image away.

"James?" Captain Mertz called again. Was it just his imagination that lent the voice an air of desperate hope that he wouldn't answer?

No, he decided. He would not be responsible for any of his fellow firefighters deaths. He removed the radio from his belt, dropped it to the roof and stomped on it. It shattered with a crunch, and he felt an odd sense of satisfaction, of peace wash through him.

It wouldn't be long now, he knew. A few minutes perhaps. Soon the rushing flames would suck the oxygen out of the air and he'd collapse. He took off his helmet, dropped it to the rooftop and sucked in a great gulp of air. Overhead, the stars were bright pinpricks of cold fire in a blanket of black, an odd, heavenly contrast for his last minutes alive.

Looking up at the sky, it crossed his mind to pray, though he was not a religious man, and he rarely attended services. He mentally shrugged — an extra prayer wouldn't make him any more or any less right with God. On the edge of the roof, the flames climbed over the eaves like eager imps. He sat down on his helmet, more tired than he could ever remember being.

The worst thing about dying would be not having Sara. They'd been married for the better part of twelve years. She'd always worried about this, about him dying in a fire. But she'd never nagged him about like some of the firefighter's wives did. She was proud of him, proud that he helped save lives and property. And she was strong.

James remembered a night three years ago when he'd slipped on the basement steps and had fallen ass over teakettle down them, snapping his right leg like a dry summer twig. He remembered his hoarse scream of agony and then . . . she was there. Holding him, calming him. She hadn't panicked, had stayed calmer than he'd thought she would. He'd been the scared one, while she had been strong and beautiful.

The fire crept closer and he smiled at his memory of that time in their lives. He'd been in a full leg cast for weeks and fooling around had been a tricky proposition. They'd managed though, and when the cast came off, they'd made up for lost time. He hadn't minded a bit.

The heat was stifling, and he could no longer see his breath.

But, he realized, he could see her. Right there on the edge of the rooftop, and he suddenly knew how scared he was, how bad he'd wanted her to hold him as he died. Through the roar of the flames, he said her name and she smiled.

Closer she came, a fire ghost, a mirage of light, he knew it had to be, but when her arms wrapped themselves around his neck in that familiar way, he could smell her perfume. "Sara," he said again. "You're here."

"Shhh," she whispered. "It's all right." Her blonde hair was curled about her face just like it did when she stepped out of the shower.

He leaned into her, the sweat on his brow forgotten, the flames — he could see them on the other side of her — a distant threat. "I'm . . . I'm sorry, Sara," he said.

"I know," she said. "I know."

"I'm scared," he admitted, inhaling the sweet fragrance of her hair. The tar on the roof was bubbling. Had her eyes always been this blue, this intense?

She smiled at him, kissed him on the lips. "Don't be," she said. "There's nothing to be scared of."

"I'm going to die, honey," he said.

The ghost Sara said nothing, kissed him again.

"Sara," James said, "I love you."

"I love you, too, Jim," she said. Then she stood and removed her robe.

For a long second he wondered why she was wearing her bathrobe with nothing on underneath, how she managed not to be sweating and soot streaked but pale and beautiful. Her lithe form was outlined by flame, but he could see her trimmed pubic thatch, her clitoris peeking from between her swollen lips. Her breasts were taut, her pink nipples hard as though she was excited by the breath of the flames surrounding her.

A hallucination, his mind answered. You're mind is taking you away from the fire.

He ignored the possibility that it wasn't real, focused on her.

"Love me, Jim," she said.

He stood, took her in his arms, his lips finding hers. Her breath was a moist, cool sensation on his tongue, and when she spoke again — "Love me, Jim" — her words were urgent inside his mouth. His hands found her naked buttocks, caressed them, then squeezed each one.

She peeled him out of his coat — it was so hot now, he could barely breathe, and what did he need with a coat anyway? — and her hands ran familiar patterns over his chest, down to his belt. He wanted her now, more desperate to be inside her and with her than he'd ever been before. The fire of the building was nothing compared to the heat at his groin, the strain of his hard shaft against the fabric of his pants. Her hands undid the buckle, and as his pants slid off his hips her hands grasped him.

He gasped — how could her hands be so cool? — and ran his hands through her hair. She stroked him firmly with one hand, while the other found his scrotum and rubbed.

God how he loved her, loved her touches. He pushed gently on her shoulders and she knelt before him, taking his full length into her mouth, and as he arched his head back, he saw the stars again, ringed with halos of light. He inhaled, and the heat seared him, burning all the way down to his roots. His mind warned him that it was almost time, almost over. Had their love making ever seemed so urgent?

James reached down and urged Sara to stand. He put his hands to either side of her pale face, memorizing her eyes, her lips, the slight line that ran just to the left of her nose. Then he reached down, and lifted her onto his swollen shaft. She gasped once as he penetrated her, her breath hot in his ear. "Yes, Jim," she hissed. "Take me right now."

He thrust upward, could barely breathe, but thrust again. Her hair was in his face, her perfume a sweet counterpoint to the smell of the burning building all around him. "I love you, Jim," she said. "I love you."

"I . . . love . . . you . . . too, Sara," he managed. It hurt now, the fire surrounding him. It hurt losing her even more. He thrust upwards, and she arched her back, crying out with the force of him inside her.

He tried to speak, but his lips were dry, chapped, and his throat — had it ever been so dry? — betrayed him. He swallowed and his throat clicked. He knew Sara wasn't here, knew she was safe at home. But her spirit was here, her love, and that's all that mattered to him in these final, thrusting seconds. He tried again, "I'm sorry, Sara," as his climax took him, his life spurting out of him, the heat causing it to evaporate before it reached the ground.

He collapsed, and still he could see her image. Her form, faint in the harsh light of the flames, curled next to him. She wrapped him in her arms, kissed him, and said, "Shhh, Jim. I know."

Her words washed over him, a cool wave passing across his burning body. He shivered. Wanted to say more, say enough. But all his strength was gone.

He wasn't hot anymore. The fire didn't burn.

James breathed once, easily. The fire offered its first delicate kiss to his clothing, which caught like summer grass.

He ignored it. Sara was here. Nothing else mattered, nothing else was real. He wasn't scared.

As the cold stars looked down upon him, he slept, cradled in a long French kiss of fire.

The Death of Winston Foster

" . . . so if you've found yourself dreaming of killing your abusive husband, take it as a sign that a significant part of you has already done the deed. It is unfortunate that the dream itself is not nearly as gratifying or effective as actually doing him in . . ."

— Maxwell Centouro, 2075 A.D.

*T*here are good days and bad days when you make your living as a police detective. Most of them, including this one, were bad. I made an effort to think about the good days as I steered my air car to the home of a recently — very recently — widowed lady by the name of Francis Foster. She knew I was coming, and from the tone of her voice when I'd called, she had already heard the news. Her husband was dead.

I'd spent the first part of my morning at the scene of the accident, which didn't get my day off to a flying start. Her husband, Winston Foster, had been killed by a hypertrain traveling at 380 miles per hour, on his way to the office. When it hit Winston Foster's car, it had spread his body like raspberry jam down the tracks and into the ditch. He'd been initially identified by a fingerprint scan from his left hand, which was attached to his left arm, which wasn't attached to anything at all. The arm had been found among the weeds in the ditch by a rookie cop who'd promptly thrown up at the sight.

The problem, and the reason I was involved at all, was that there are numerous safety systems built into a car to prevent just such an occurrence. I had been assigned the rather grim task of breaking the news to Mrs. Foster, as well as investigating what — if any — reasons might exist for the accident. All in all, it was building up to be a banner bad day.

I arrived at her home, parked the air car on the pad, and walked to her door. The house was beautiful. Maroon colored plasi-bricks lined the walkways and flawless ivy crawled up the chimney. I palmed the touch pad next to the door. A feminine-computer voice said, "Identify please."

Yep, I thought, definitely wealthy to afford this kind of security system. "Bridges, Jacob R.," I said. "Detective 1st class, Omaha Police Department."

The pleasant, if slightly metallic, voice responded, "Please wait."

I stood there for a moment while the computer ran a check against my hand print and did a voice analysis. Finally, "Identity confirmed. Please stand by."

"Please come in, detective," Mrs. Foster said over the security speaker. Her voice automatically triggered the door locks.

I stepped through the doorway, and I heard her say, "Come to the dining room please. Straight down the hallway on your right."

I followed her directions to the dining room and saw her standing, dry-eyed, next to the mahogany dining table. We stood there looking at each other, and I could see that she'd been crying earlier even if she wasn't now. She had a look of concentration in her large brown eyes as she absently fingered an overripe plum from the fruit basket on the table. A slight smile lingered around the corners of her mouth. I could tell she was assessing me, and I was suddenly reminded of a wild animal testing the air for signs of danger.

"Mrs. Foster, I'm Detective Bridges, Omaha P.D.," I said, extending my hand.

"Yes, I know," she said. "The security system said so, and I recognize your voice from your call earlier, of course."

"I see," I said. "Mrs. Foster, I'm sorry to have to tell you this, but — "

She held up a hand. "I know. Winston died in a hypertrain accident at approximately 8:13 this morning." Her voice seemed rote, as though she were hypnotized or in a trance.

I nodded, having expected this. Still, I was curious. "How did you find out?" I asked.

"Oh, there's no mystery there, detective. I know because I killed him."

I stood there, my jaw hanging somewhere between my belt and my knees. "I beg your pardon?" I asked.

"I said I killed him," she repeated, sounding vaguely annoyed.

Trying to catch up, and assuming that this was her grief talking, I said, "How did you do that, Mrs. Foster?"

She waved her hands at me in exasperation. "Listen, detective. Why don't we get down to brass tacks? This isn't me feeling guilty or upset that he's dead. I don't. In fact, I'm relieved.

"The simple fact is that I killed him. Unfortunately, my confession is null and void because I could be grief stricken right now. I don't have my attorney present. I couldn't possibly know what I'm saying. All of which leads me to ask you something. Do you want to hear the story, or just take me downtown and have me released within the day?"

A lot of detective work depends on instinct and intuition. Trusting your gut feelings. At that moment, my gut had a sinking feeling in it that made me want to sit down and put my head between my knees. I took a deep breath and made an effort to control myself. I could tell she was serious, but I could also tell she was scared. I shook my head in bewilderment. How in the world, I thought, do you kill someone with a hypertrain? She must be delusional or something. "O.k., Mrs. Foster, why don't you tell me the whole story?" I asked.

"I'm a ms. now," she said. "You may, if you choose, call me Fran."

"All right, Fran. I'll listen to what you have to say," I said.

"One condition," she said. "After you've heard my story, you'll have to decide whether or not you want to arrest me. That means I want as fair a hearing from you as possible — meaning no interruptions, no questions, and," she pointed at me and tugged her earlobe, "no recordings. I know that police have a recording chip built in. If you understand what you hear, you file a report that clears me. If you don't, I'll come with you and confess for real."

She was one gutsy lady, I had to give her that. And I was intrigued. I'd only heard of one other case of a car hitting a hypertrain, and that was because the driver had smashed into it on purpose. Normally, the automatic breaking system would stop the vehicle before it even tapped the blocking bar to the tracks. If she really had killed him, how had she done it? Still, I couldn't promise the moon.

"Just a second, Fran. I'll agree to everything you said, but I can't promise not to arrest you. I'm a cop, not a judge, remember? But I'll listen to your story, and we'll go from there. And I have a condition, too," I added.

She looked at me suspiciously, and I realized that Frannie Foster knew all the rules of the game. She knew I had to file a report on what I'd learned. She also knew that sometimes, given a good enough reason, a cop would lie.

"What's that?" she asked.

I smiled at her. "Call me Jacob," I said. I thought a soft touch interview would draw her out. If I scared her, she'd probably just freeze on me and then I'd be stuck.

She nodded. "I'll get us some coffee," she said, and turned away, heading for the kitchen area. "I gave the servant the day off."

I took the opportunity to really assess her. The vision chip I used told me she was 5.531 feet tall and weighed 110.223 pounds in her current clothing. She was small, almost tiny compared to me. She carried herself in a defensive manner, as though at any moment she expected to be rebuked or maybe tackled. She was also, I thought, quite pretty. I really couldn't picture her plotting murder. But it's always the ones you least suspect.

As she reentered the room, backing through the swinging partition between the kitchen and the dining room and holding a tray with two coffee cups on it, I attempted to ask a question. Pulling out my palm-top, I said, "Fran, could I ask about Mr. — "

She turned so quickly that she nearly spilled the coffee. "I said 'no questions' and I meant it," she snapped.

"Whoa, hold on a minute!" I said. "You're going to have to give me a break here. First, I'm a cop and that's part of my job. If I'm going to understand everything, I need some background."

Her shoulders sagged a little. "You're right, of course," she said. "I'm sorry, Jacob. It's just, well, I need to do this in my own way." She smiled ruefully and shrugged. "Ask your questions then, but please, be brief. I don't really know if I have the strength to tell this twice."

"No problem. I just wanted to clarify the events of this morning. Sort of set the end in sight, so I can see where we're going."

She shrugged again, and said, "O.k."

"Why don't you start by telling me a little about your husband? What was he like?" I asked.

She didn't say anything for nearly a full minute, but I waited. I didn't want to set her off again. I wanted her story, but I wanted it coherent. Her eyes were cast down and to the left, body language that told me she was remembering something.

Softly, so soft that her voice had changed almost entirely, she said, "Big."

"I beg your pardon?" I asked.

"He was big. A big man, very strong. Very smart. He was an investment banker."

I knew all that, of course, from the crime scene and arm scan this morning as well as the preliminary computer report I'd run on Mr. Foster. Still, it was a start.

"Did he say anything to you this morning before he left? Something to make you angry?"

"No," she giggled a little under her breath. "He told me to take out the garbage." She was still remembering, not looking at me directly. "I guess I did," she said.

Wanting to catch her in this reflective mood, I quietly asked, "Did you really kill your husband, Fran?"

"Oh yes, Detective Jacob Bridges. I killed him in self-defense."

For the second time that morning, I sat there dumbfounded. Self-defense? How the hell do you kill someone in self-defense with a hypertrain? She laughed again, lightly, and waited for my reply. Finally, I said, "Self-defense, huh? I guess you'll have to explain that one to me."

"I know," she said. "And that's the story I'm going to tell you. The story you need to hear."

"Well then, I guess I'm done asking questions. At least for now."

"Very well," she said, "then I can begin."

Her eyes went down-left again, and we both ignored the coffee. Her soft melodic voice was the only sound in the room. She said, "It all goes back to an anonymous e-mail I received last summer. It said that the person knew I was an abused wife, and if I wanted to get out of the situation, I should come to a secure virtual chat to hear this man speak.

"Winston would've killed me if he'd known. But I went anyway. By then, I was so desperate for a way out that I would've done anything at all. The one time I tried to stop him, he beat the hell out of me. Of course, he knew a judge so the matter just 'disappeared' from the official records." She laughed bitterly. "Still, I thought maybe this chat was my last hope. So I went."

I nodded, and said, "I understand what you must've been feeling. My sister was abused. It only ended when my father died. What happened at the chat?" I asked.

"My whole life changed," she said.

"*I* sat in the 14th row of the dark auditorium and

wondered what I was doing. I stopped there by accident really, or maybe it was curiosity. Hope is not something I was feeling. Mostly, I was afraid that my husband would come home while I was online and plug in to see what I was doing.

"The speaker was a blond man, in his early 30's. He was dressed in a cream colored sweater and blue jeans. I remember because he seemed so confident and relaxed. His voice wasn't deep, but he spoke well. I thought he sounded like a minister."

"Ladies," he said, "my name is Maxwell Centouro. I am here to help you, and if you listen to me, your troubles — at least those with your husbands — will soon be over.

"My father was an alcoholic and an abuser. On the last night of his wretched life, he beat my mother for the very last time. Because he killed her. And I killed him.

"What I didn't know at the time was this: I should have done it in such a way as to leave no doubt that it was an accident. But I didn't. Instead, I got sent to prison for seven long years. But while I was there, I made one vow to myself. When I got out, I would teach others — women like yourselves, whose husbands hurt them — how to escape the situation."

"I remember thinking at the time that it was like a dream. Winston would never allow me to escape. Never allow me to leave him. Still, I listened. It seemed I had no choice."

"You can't rely on the law, ladies. My mom tried that. And he won't get better if you just do the right thing. All he will do is get worse and worse. Because he likes hurting you. And I'm here today to teach you how to stop him."

"I remember how silent it was in that room. All around me the women were completely quiet, though a few of them cried softly to themselves as Maxwell talked. They sounded like wounded animals. I probably would have left then, but I was already hooked. I felt hope again.

"Winston hit me all the time, and every time it got worse. I would've left but for one thing. Something so small that Winston had already forgotten it, I'm sure. Two weeks before I happened into this lecture, Winston had beat me with a belt in this very room. Not far from where you're sitting, Jacob.

"And as I laid on the floor, crying and begging for him to stop, he stood over me with that damn belt in his hand and he smiled. He was enjoying my misery. I realized then that I'd do anything to be free of that smile for the rest of my life.

"I learned a lot that day. I learned that it must appear to be an accident, and just in case, to document the abuse. I also learned four techniques that Maxwell said would 'take care of your husband permanently'. The best one for me, or rather for Winston, was number three. Maxwell called it: For the man who has a daily pattern. It was perfect.

"You see, Jacob, Winston had a pattern. Was a man in love with patterns. If I let him fall behind schedule for any reason, his wrath was terrifying. So I planned a way to use it against him.

"It took me six months to figure it out. To find the "hole" in his pattern where an accident could happen. It took me another three months of online study to figure out how to make the accident happen. During this time, I documented as much as I could about what Winston was doing to me. I took pictures and wrote everything down. My biggest fear was that he would find them."

I finally interrupted. "Hold on a minute. Do you still have those pictures and stuff?"

"Yes," she said, "I do. Maxwell taught us very well. But I thought we'd agreed on no more questions?"

"You're right," I said. "Sorry, go ahead." I noticed when she spoke her voice automatically lowered in tone. Another body language sign of submission.

She continued, "Of course, he beat me during those months. But in some ways it was worth it. For the first time in nine long years I had a secret. Something Winston didn't know. I think, maybe, that a mad little part of me was in love with the very idea of secrecy. Of having something to myself. I hid the pictures and letters under the grill vent of the refrigerator. And I watched Winston.

"Each day, I learned more about his schedule. Finally, I spotted the hole. He insisted on driving to work. In that ridiculous 'classic' car of his, rather than take an air car or use the city train. Every morning at 8:04 sharp, Winston left for work. Not at 8:05, and not at 8:03. As I said, he was really stuck on his schedule.

"The hypertrain crosses the tracks at 8:13. I know because I timed it every damn day for a month. I told Winston I wanted to lose some weight, so I left the house right at 8:00 to bicycle down there and check the time. It was hell, Jacob, to get on the bike and pedal like crazy in order to get there and be away before Winston drove by.

"Always, the train got there at 8:13. So, just like Winston, the hypertrains ran on time. I just needed to get him there at the right time. And he needed to be distracted, just enough to take his mind of the train and his car. It wasn't that difficult really. Once I figured it out, I was surprised that I hadn't thought of it sooner." Her voice trailed off, and she looked at me. "Jacob, do you ever feel that way?" she asked.

"Yeah, Fran, sometimes I do. Like now, except I don't have all the answers yet. How did you do it?"

"I set his watch back. His big, fancy watch that could tell him right down to the second what time it was."

I knew the watch, having seen it that morning. "O.k., but what made him crash?"

"Simple. Last night, while he slept, I went out to the garage to accomplish two things that I learned. You see, what I studied online during those months was mechanics. 'Classic Vehicle Maintenance 101' was the actual course title," she said.

I looked at her with some admiration. "You shorted the automatic breaking system, didn't you?" I asked.

She smiled proudly for a moment, and nodded. "Yes I did. It was really easy. All the older cars had the system wired in as an after market product. It wasn't something back then that the manufacturers put in."

"What was the second thing?" I asked. "You said 'two things'."

"Oh yes. The distraction. His 'classic' car is — was — air-cooled. I sprayed mace into the vents on the front of his windshield, and on his hood. When it pulls air in from the outside, I guessed that it would pull the spray in, too."

"But how could you know he would turn on the air inside the car?" I objected.

"I couldn't. I took a gamble that it would be another hot day and it paid off. I estimated that as soon as he was out of the driveway, he would turn on the air. It takes about 7 minutes to cycle the air system into full operation. I guessed that the spray would hit him about 60 seconds before he crossed the tracks. I assume it did."

I sat there for a few minutes, saying nothing. It was stunning how she'd worked it out. Essentially, she'd made his eyes water just seconds before he would cross the tracks. The tracks were at the bottom of an steep hill and surrounded by a ditch on either side. Even if the spray hadn't worked, he probably would have crashed with no breaks at that speed. Had he left at his normal time, the train would have been there and gone before him. I had to admire it.

I looked at her, and could see the desperate hope on her face. "Can I see those pictures, please?" I asked.

"Sure," she said, and rose to go get them. When she returned, she tossed me a large envelope. Inside were pictures of her bruised body. In one photo, I could see welt marks on her ribs from a strap or a belt of some kind. In another, there were cigar shaped burns on the inside of her thighs. I shuddered. It was enough.

Smiling at her, I said, "Sorry about your husband, Fran."

"Yes," she said, "thank you." This time her smile was real. "It's a shame he had to go that way, but at least he felt no pain."

"You're a generous woman, Fran. He deserved far worse than what he got."

"I know," she said, "but accidents happen."

I left the home of Francis Foster, and got back in my air car. As the autodrive engaged, I reported in to the station that I was headed home for lunch, and that I would report in later. I listened to her story on my ear chip as the traffic flew by.

The air car landed on the roof pad of the apartment building where I lived. Walking down the steps, I erased the recording I'd made of Fran's story. I believed her, Foster was an abuser of the highest order, and I'd promised her no recordings. I entered my apartment and tossed my coat on the kitchen table.

I ordered up a sandwich and a beer from the auto-chef. While it was synthesizing my lunch, I turned on my computer system. Grabbing my meal, I sat down at my console and plugged myself in through the neural jack on the back of my skull. Entering virtual reality has always been a pleasant escape for me.

Soaring over numerous sites, I activated my security program, and located the chat "room" where I spent most of my spare time. I stepped in, and looked out into the room. It was, in actuality, an auditorium. Filled with women.

There are good days and bad days when you make your living as a police detective. Today had turned out pretty well.

I stepped out onto the auditorium stage, and said, "Ladies, my name is Maxwell Centouro. I am here to help you, and if you listen to me, your troubles — at least those with your husbands — will soon be over..."

PART THREE
Traveler

Traveler

for L.L.

And when you left home,
there was always the drum-song,
a message from Alaska
calling to you from the soil
under your booted feet.

On this map, distance is a
deception, alone you told
your story to cedars and pines,
animals whose live you couldn't know:
a raven, a wolf, a lemming.
The air held your breath in
cloud memory, brief moments of
permafrost focus.

You found the old man healer
north of Fairbanks, and he told
you the story of a late-spring
blizzard, something temporary.
Sharing coffee, he spoke of tundra
grass journeys he took as a boy.

After carving a pipe, he sent you
away on the crooked path home.

Passing through the Mulchatna salmon
river, mountain ranges and grasslands
filled with wind and fire,
you travel the uneven blood waters
of your wrist. You don't use a
compass, or the map engraved on the
soles of your broken boots.

And when you returned home,
there was always the drum-song,
a message from the soil
your feet first touched, reminding
you that a circle has no ends,
and that we are travelers —
leaving or returning to
the unlikely geography
of our still beating hearts, to
find that we are alive.

The Morality of Feeling Good

" ... I heard of an old man who saw only grays —
he fell in love for the first time, saw yellows,
and it stopped his heart.
They buried him on a Thursday ... "

— Of Memory

*T*he Age of Information is ending.
    Sitting here in the dimly lit Oval Office and trying to decide how damning my signature on this law will be is an ending of sorts, too, though it's safe to assume that the Internet, or the Net as it's now called, will always exist in some form or another. But the price of all that free floating information is going to be paid. No one ever imagined it could go so far, so fast. No one, at least not the creative geniuses behind the whole thing, thought twice about the ramifications of a virtual world where anything and everything, every bit and byte of information was available to anyone. Some of it was for the good — medical science improved by

leaps and bounds, instant communication between peoples and cultures tore down walls that the politicians could never breach in their wildest, wettest diplomatic dreams, and the knowledge — virtual libraries more vast than any paper-based collection — provided previously unimaginable opportunities for research. But the bad stuff...

The bad stuff spread like instant cancer, like AIDS. You could start out with a simple search, "WORLD WAR II" and end up, quite by accident, at a site on "HOW TO MAKE YOUR OWN THERMONUCLEAR DEVICE." Even that might have been acceptable — along with the sites for gambling, the sites for hiring mercenaries, and probably even the sites describing "101 WAYS TO SERVE LABRADOR RETRIEVER." These all might have been ok, some people would have grumbled, some would have cried out in dismay "What about the CHILDREN???!!," but all might have passed except for one thing, the obvious thing. Our darkest dreams, our most fathomless passion: sex.

Sex was everywhere on the Net. And even this might have been acceptable, but for the vast array (and I'm falling somewhat into opinion country here) of sick, twisted, perverted, absolutely unacceptable forms of sexual pleasure. If you could think it, you could find it. One study of Net-based image groups found a site where people were getting their jollies by watching images of naked women in metal boots crush the life out of small animals. Everything from erotic asphyxiation to water sports. Step right up, folks and pick your perversion. And it went too far, too fast, and it was accessible. To the CHILDREN! To anyone with a computer. It wasn't all like that, but we had to stop it, didn't we?

In so many ways, we have become a country so set

on being politically correct, on doing the right thing, that we'll do anything — so long as we do it right now — that we never see how the pendulum gains momentum. Once, our country discriminated against women — less pay for the same job (if they could even get the same job), poor treatment in the workforce, fewer benefits — you probably remember this. And we acted. We passed laws, we jumped up and down, we yelled and screamed and eventually, the pendulum began to swing. We couldn't foresee the consequences of our actions — the radical shift in what had always been the foundation of our society, the family — suddenly finding itself without either parent at home; the changes in the economic structure of our country; or even the fact that (like any pendulum in motion) energy gathers energy, power hungers for itself.

So the sex . . . it was out there. At first, just pictures. Then sound. Then video, and video with sound, and so on to the point where you could virtually meet, talk, flirt, buy dinner, go dancing, invite her up for coffee, and fuck her on your sofa — and wouldn't ever have to worry about RESPECT in the morning — and you could do it, pun intended, anonymously. Slip on a virtual headset, and you could stroke yourself right into the digital lust machine of the future. But it reached the breaking point, and we had to stop it. Rather, I had to stop it.

And so I introduced the legislation, called the Internet Sex Abolition Act, or the ISAA, into the House of Representatives, and with a little nudge here, and a little push there, it passed and went on to the Senate. And, you can guess this one, can't you — those conservative good old boys just loved it. I don't have to tell you that at their age most of those gentlemen wouldn't know what to do with sex in the real world, let alone a virtual lay. And it passed. Damn near exactly how I'd written it.

And now here it is. On my desk. Waiting for a signature, while outside the news crews wait like buzzards. Because they know. They know it all. And they would just love to pick my carcass clean to the bone.

During the final phase of my run for the White House, my wife died. Suddenly, and without any warning, her heart gave out, and not only was I a widower, but I was a practical shoe-in for the Presidency of the United States of America. My campaign manager, Brenda Hugh, said, "There's nothing in the world like a sympathy vote. You could practically screw goats on your front lawn and still win." (Now it sort of makes me wonder what websites she'd been surfing at the time.) But she was right. It was a landslide. And I didn't even have to have sex with the goats.

But the key to this . . . present dilemma, you must understand, was that I loved my wife in the most profound sense. And without this knowledge, how I ended up here and why I'm having am internal debate over signing my own legislation, wouldn't make a great deal of sense. We made a great team, and our marriage was based on two simple things: we could present a charismatic couple to the political world at large, and the people (who are mostly sheep, or goats, depending on your point of view), would eat it up. Publicly, we made John and Jackie look like a couple of hacks. The second reason, and much more private, was that our personal life — and in particular our sex life — was wonderful. In touching each other, we found solace, a safe harbor in the often stormy seas of public life, and we knew each other as only people who are committed to fully exploring each other can.

Our private activities were the fuel that gave us enough passion to pursue life in public together. In addition to our marriage vows, we made a commitment to each other professionally and politically. I wanted to be President, and she knew that the role of First Lady could be a hell of a lot more powerful than just hosting tea luncheons for visiting dignitary's wives. Our shared passions — private pleasure together and public power — took a long time to achieve, but we got there. First at the state level, when I won the race for Governor of Massachusetts, then the Senate, and finally, the White House. But to that bastion of power, I went alone. She was already buried.

And without her partnership, I came to realize the horrible truth. My life, my personal life, was gray. Gray like rain on the Mississippi, or dew on concrete. In my life, I had only loved her, and I'd never really looked to anyone else. I'd gone to her funeral, and the lowering of her casket into the cold ground that late August day seemed to leave me passionless and exhausted. I watched, but I didn't, if you know what I mean. Was it Poe who said "All that we see or seem is but a dream within a dream?" Lust is easy, but love. . . ? No, love hadn't seemed possible to me then. From then on, I was alone and the days and weeks and months of my life flew by, and I was still cold. And no one is really alone like the President.

Two years after I'd sworn the Oath of Office for the first time, I started spending time online. I didn't know if time had finally healed the wounds, or if I had become simply desperate to find a reason to feel good again. It's possible that I began looking because more than anything, I had started to feel old and broken. Wanting something or someone that could color my existence. (Which explains, if nothing else, my passing familiarity with the full spectrum of available Net perversions. You can't go anywhere, even vaguely related to sex, and not see this stuff.) It's not like it was in Kennedy's day, when the press was at least a little discreet. Hell, it's not even like it was in Clinton's day, when you couldn't even break wind (let alone boff an intern with a cigar) without it winding up as commentary on a Sunday morning news show. It's far, far worse — thanks to Clinton and that buffoon who followed him, the President can't even go out on a date. So while I was out on the Net looking for someone that could, if nothing else, replace the gray void in my heart, they were watching me. And seeing nothing. My handle CMDRNCHIEF generated a lot of chat room laughs, but no one suspected, no one knew.

And then I met her. And my world, gray for so long, became a rainbow.

Our relationship started in the privacy of the virtual world, where no one called me "Mr. President," and everything is as real or unreal as your imagination can make it. Sitting in the privacy of my White House bedroom, my virtual headset in place, I wandered into a chat room for singles.

"Hello, CMDRNCHIEF," she said.

"Hello," I said.

It's worth noting here that in the virtual world, the need for typing, one-handed or otherwise, has long since disappeared. Now, you just talk and the Net carries the sound into the digital infinity and plays it for your listener.

"I'm 1LONLYREDHEAD," she said.

"So, I see," I said back. "And are you?"

"Lonely?" she asked.

"No," I laughed, "a redhead?" My wife had been a

redhead. Her name was Dara. She was two years dead and why should I feel this flurry of guilt? Were all redheads as fiery and passionate as my late wife? I doubted it.

"Yes, I am," she said. "The real thing, too."

"That sounds . . . nice," I said.

"And are you?" she asked.

"Am I what?"

"A commander in chief? Is that a euphemism for CEO?"

"Something like that," I said.

I'd like to tell you that we had cheap virtual sex, but if I did, I'd be lying. Nor would I be in the predicament I'm currently in. Of course, if we had, then maybe my world would still be gray.

We talked for two hours that first night, chatting away in an online café, sipping virtual coffee, and discovering that while we were both lonely, we shared other interests, too. We never exchanged names. Anonymity is both the bane and the blessing of the Internet. We agreed to meet again.

And so it went. It was a year before we worked out virtual constructs of ourselves, rather than the standard interfaces that were all pretty much the same. For her it was expensive, and for me, nearly impossible. I couldn't just give her an image of me, yet I didn't want to lie either. The other problem was hiring a programmer to design it who wouldn't blab at the first sign of a check from a tabloid. I managed to work around the problem — using the whole Net anonymity thing as a shield.

Once we had "seen" each other, it wasn't long before we were doing all kinds of virtual activities together — sky surfing, watching movies, you name it — but mostly we just walked and talked. She is beautiful, and I trust that her virtual self is accurate to the real thing.

Her red hair hangs in lovely curls and ringlets down to her shoulders, and her body is well formed: curves in all the right places, her breasts large enough to draw the eye (and the hand!) but no so large as to be a permanent distraction. Her voice is soft, with a hint of a southern accent. I cannot, of course, smell her, though I imagine fresh mown grass, or lilac.

We talked of many things, but rarely ourselves. We didn't bother to explore what the other person did for a living, or where we lived in the real world. These things seemed petty somehow, unimportant. We didn't exchange real names, she was "Red" and I was "Chief."

We dated for two years on the Net, and I was back on the campaign trail for my second term, when we nearly fell. Oh, we'd fooled around a little — virtual kissing, a little petting, but that night — I was in a hotel in Georgia and we had thought to go all the way. Virtual longing had long since been replaced by virtual lust. I wanted her. To taste her in the only way I could. To hold her virtual form in my hands and mold her flesh with the patterns of my pleasure, while in the real world I stroked myself to a jolting climax.

The virtual hotel room was small and cramped and hot, but it would suffice. We had waited and wanted long enough. And before I even had my shoes off she was touching me, licking me, stroking my chest and removing my clothes. My hands found her breasts, and though it had been a long time since I'd touched the real thing, virtually I was an apparent pro. Through the thin veneer of her sweater, I found and lightly pinched her nipples.

We fell back on the bed, our breath coming in little gasps and moans. I removed her top, then her bra, and her breasts came forth, magnificent orbs longing to be kissed. I obliged, using my tongue on the areolas before finding the nipples, hard and ripe.

Her hands pulled my shirt loose from my pants, removed it, and she proceeded to post a rain of kisses, nips, and licks down my face, neck, and across my chest.

In the hotel in Georgia, I stroked a little faster. God how I wanted her, but she never pressed me to meet. In person we could be so much more, do so much more...

Then our pants were off, final undergarments cast aside. I rolled on top of her, ready to enter her. I could feel the heat coming off her wet crotch in waves. I could see the little freckles on her skin, miniature contrasts to the pale milk of her complexion. I was going to bury myself in her to the hilt. Be surrounded by her. Take her and be taken by her. She was so soft, warm and beautiful; her green eyes were closed in a gesture of passion and concentration.

And just as I was about to thrust forward, she said, "Stop!"

And I did, though how I'm not certain. I thought that I would explode right then, from the wanting. In my Georgia hotel room, I could feel my penis throbbing in my hand, begging for release. My balls ached.

"What?" I asked. "Why?"

She was gasping, wanting, too. "Because we can't. We can't."

Desperate now, like any man driven to the pinnacle of pleasure, still not getting it, I said, "Why?"

She smiled. "Because we're not married." She looked at me seriously. "I won't have sex until I'm married, virtual reality or real world."

"Oh," I said, feeling myself wilt a little. "Oh." And I grew silent then, looking down on her prone form and feeling the old guilt spring forth again. She was right. She wasn't my wife.

"I'm sorry," she said. "It's just that..."

"No," I said. "You're right. We don't even know each other." In my excitement, I had lost sight of this formality, important as it was. It's a great deal harder to think clearly with your dick in your hand. And she was right.

She laughed. "Of course we do! Only virtually, of course, but we know each other. And we can do other things until then . . . if it happens." And she slid down the length of my body, took me in her mouth, and I for a time I forgot all about marriage. For a time, I lost myself in her as I had once lost myself in my wife.

She played me masterfully, one minute her mouth a warm, wet cave of air, the next, her tongue licking the very tip of my shaft. She rotated on the bed, slipping a leg over my face. And I tasted her. Reveled in the press of her thighs against my cheeks, the little moans she released when I found her clit and sucked it between my teeth.

She ran her hands down my legs, and back up again to cup my balls, one finger pressed to that ultra sensitive spot just beneath the sack, her nail scratching lightly. I could hear the sound of my cock sliding into her mouth, and it urged me on. She pressed back against my mouth, wanting my tongue, and I gave it to her. We pushed against each other, the rhythm intoxicating, holding tight as we climbed toward an explosion.

In the hotel room in Georgia, I prayed for no interruptions, no national emergencies, while I stroked myself like a mad banjo player. I wondered where she was in the real world, what her hands were doing to herself as she laid on her bed, or sat in a computer console. How wet she must be as she fingered her engorged clitoris.

And this thought pushed me over the edge in both worlds. I surged against my hand, against her mouth at the same time, the tempo of my tongue on her virtual body reaching a crescendo, and she cried out against me, her body wracked by the spasm of her orgasm. We came together, lost in each other in a world that didn't exist, lost, perhaps, in ourselves, in a world that shouldn't.

It was a wonderful moment, a wonderful ecstasy to be with her. And it made things so much more complicated. Because my wife was dead and I still felt guilty, because the whole Net sex thing had to be stopped, because I realized that I loved her.

She asked me that night, after it was over and we lay side by side on the virtual bed. "Do you want to get married?"

I admired her for that. She hadn't asked me while she was stroking my shaft with her lips. I sighed. "I can't," I said.

"Why?" she asked. "Are you already married?"

"No," I said. "My wife died a few years ago."

"Then why?"

"Because my situation prevents it," I said, sounding to myself and undoubtedly to her, like someone who would rather dodge a question than answer it. I tried again. "I love you, Red," I said. "I really do. But I can't get married — virtually, or in the real world."

"I see," she said. But she didn't. And I had hurt her.

"Maybe we should meet for real," she said.

"I can't do that either, Red," I said. "I'm sorry."

If this were the only predicament I were in, then I would have said to hell with the whole thing, and just met her. Gone on a date like a real person maybe, and let the press take their pictures and make their suppositions. But that was before the other shoe dropped.

I got caught.

A clever reporter from the Times, one James Thibodaux, started thinking that if the President didn't date, then maybe, just maybe, he was spending his private time online. And with the help of a hacker named Raven (whose first name — Hershel — seems both strange and ominous to me) managed to track me down, one digital trail at a time.

And when the story broke, some three weeks after I'd sent the legislation to Congress, I found myself in an irredeemable situation. It wasn't indefensible, quite the contrary, as we could put spin on it all day long. And while they'd tracked me, they hadn't found Red. I couldn't either because at this point, going online and into the virtual world would be political suicide.

I wanted to see her. I suspected she knew who I was, and had wisely gone into hiding. I loved her, needed to talk to her, tell her how sorry I was that — in the end — I had lied. But she was nowhere to be found. And the press, once they had figured out the Net angle, were everywhere.

Two politicians, whose names (and now their careers) don't really matter, got caught in a virtual spanking scenario.

A few more were sighted attending a virtual orgy.

Others, whose personal perversions aren't worth mention, were seen.

Everyone was tracked. Everyone was watched. And the reaction to the ISAA Bill was fast and furious. If the leaders of the free world were engaging in this kind of thing, it had to be stopped. For the children.

So here I am. Sitting at my desk in the oval office. I am without her, and my world is doing a slow fade to gray. I have to sign the ISAA Bill into law. I introduced it — my thought at the time was that it really had gone way too far. And in some ways, it had.

But I never thought about the adults. The people who were capable of making decisions about their sex lives, and accepting responsibility for those decisions. I never thought about the adults, who should have protected the children better, and who could have, and none of this would have been necessary.

We could have had a virtual playground where every sexual desire — both the accepted and the bizarre — was ours for the taking. In safety and without fear of diseases or social repercussions. Our desires, from the mundane to the monstrous, would have been anonymous, clean and safe. How wonderful. And how horrible that I hadn't thought of that before, safe in a cocoon of my own sanctity about what was acceptable.

But I was caught by my own ingenuity, my own fears of sex, just like the rest of the western world — confused and uncertain about the morality of feeling good. And I have to sign the law. She is gone, her red hair is not even a flash on the horizon, and she is gone. I have to sign the law, or I'm worse than a hypocrite.

As I pick up my pen, I feel it. The first twinge of pain racing down my left arm. I hurry to finish this, finish both. She is gone, and I must sign the law.

Will it be dark on the other side? Will she be there? In heaven, if that's where I'm bound, what will be acceptable desire?

I sign the law.

And I wait for the pain.

The End of Summer

Carrion birds circled on thermals above the battlefield. Hundreds of foot soldiers, the last tattered remnants of the warband, lay dead or dying. The birds were waiting only for the last twitches of movement to stop, and the groans to cease. In the distance, the great castle of Camelot stood silent vigil over the ground where Arthur had made his final stand. In the fading gray sunlight of late afternoon, the walls themselves appeared to be mourning his passing. I watched as Queen Gwynevre made her slow way towards the battlefield along the road leading to the castle. She was riding her favorite horse, a bad tempered milk white stallion. Her gaze was fixed on the silhouetted figure of a large man walking towards her. Lancelot. He was limping slightly on his left leg, and still carried his shield and sword. They met at the halfway point between the castle and the field. I remained where I was, hidden in the trees, to watch.

Lancelot spoke first. "My lady, it is finished."

Her eyes flicked over the bodies littered between the river and herself. "And Arthur?" she asked softly.

"No, my lady," Lancelot said. "He fought well, but

died at the climax of the battle. It was Modred's spear that took him." As her face momentarily sharpened, he added, "It was very quick, my lady. And he killed Modred at the same exact moment, so justice was done."

She nodded, always the composed Queen. I can remember Arthur teaching her that there was always time for grief — in private. "Now what will we do, Lancelot?"

"My lady?"

"You heard me," she said.

"It is over. Modred is dead and can trouble us no more. But the warband is destroyed. And the King, my King, is dead."

"Yes, that is so," she said, while I marveled at her calm. "But what will happen to Camelot, to Britain? Will the realm survive? Will I still be Queen?"

I chose that moment to answer her from the shadows of the trees. "Of course not."

They both turned towards me in surprise. I was exhausted and no doubt looking my age. Gwynevre had a look of distaste on her face as she did whenever an elderly person was around. She was incredibly vain, and no doubt feared that the wrinkles of old age might somehow be contagious. Still, I could never fault her manners. "God be praised!" she said, as I staggered my way towards her. "Merlin, you're alive!"

"Oh, yes, Queen Gwynevre," I said. "Still quite alive, much to the chagrin of many." I looked at the battlefield and in memory replayed my part in it. "It would take worse than this pitiful battle to kill Merlin," I said.

"Still, it must be by the grace of God that you live," said Lancelot. "I thought I saw you during the battle, though perhaps I was mistaken."

"You are not mistaken. I fought in the battle, not far from Arthur's side." Here I paused to let the words sink in, and Lancelot paled somewhat. "Still," I continued, "Arthur is dead. The Kingdom of Summer has come to its end, as do all things. There will be much strife, much chaos. And there will never be another like Arthur." I turned back to Gwynevre. "You asked what will happen, my lady?"

She appeared almost eager. "Yes, Merlin. What will happen now?"

I looked at her then, to try and judge with my eyes what had become of the black-haired girl who had come here so long ago. She was not a girl now, but a woman grown both in body and in power. Her hair, once black as jet, carried a large streak of whiteness from the crown of her head. Her eyes were a pale blue today, but I'd seen them range from that to almost lavender on various occasions. She had become comfortable with power, perhaps too comfortable. It would be best if I shattered her quickly forming image of the future now, I judged. "Well," I said, "it seems a little late for the asking, but as you wish to know, I will tell you what I see."

The vision fell upon me then, and the voice that spoke next was my own and yet not my own. "I see Britain falling apart, a land torn asunder and entering into a darkness where once again barbarians plunder at will. I see the light of God dimming in the land, the trees having no leaves, and the fields bearing no harvest. Animals will starve and children will die. Camelot shall be lost, a home for ravens and jackals. And I see death. Death, plague, and fire," I said, shuddering. It was a hideous vision, but when the sight comes and places the words of the future on the tongue of a true bard, he cannot fail to utter it. As my vision cleared, I said, bitterly, "Is this the vision you hoped to hear, my Queen?"

Gwynevre paled under the onslaught, and Lancelot

had stiffened and half-raised his sword to ward off an unseen blow. "Surely, Merlin, it is not as bad as all that," she said. "There must be some hope."

"Hope, my lady?" I asked. "There is always hope."

Lancelot looked up with interest, and turned towards me. "What would that be?" he asked, with that slight sneer of his. Oh, he was an arrogant bastard for all of his greatness as a knight. Now, even that was ruined.

"Justice and bard's tales," I said. "In these lie Britain's only hope."

Gwynevre stared at me. In the last glimmer of sunlight, her hair had taken on the color of blood. "What do you mean, Merlin?" she asked.

"Yes, Merlin," Lancelot seconded. "Tell us what you mean. Don't give us your normal gibberish and riddles. Give us answers!"

"Oh, bother!" I said. "You see, yet you are blind. You hear, yet fail to listen. Must I teach you everything, now that all is lost to you? Are you children that must be guided through the dark time of night by the hand?"

Gwynevre laughed suddenly, perhaps caught up in the image of herself and Lancelot being led by me though the darkness. In that moment, I was almost able to forgive her. Her laughter was girlish and light, and dispelled the growing tension around us, at least momentarily. "Come now, Merlin," she said, "You are being unfair, my old friend. When have we done a wrong?"

And that tore it for me, but I knew the game I played and laughed anyway. "Wrong?" I asked. "Bah! Lady you have wronged so many it is a wonder that the dead of Britain do not rise up to strike you down where you stand! All of heaven cries out for justice and you wish me to absolve you? Now of all times?"

Gwynevre gasped. "What do you mean?"

"I know!" I said, bitterly. "I know about you! About

both of you! Arthur knew, and said nothing out of love for you. Worse still," I added, pointing at Lancelot, "I know the secret of his heart that not even you share at this moment."

Lancelot flushed, and his hand unconsciously dropped toward his sword hilt. I turned to face him, and raised a hand in warning. "Beware, knight. Though your prowess would surely test me, there is no doubt about who would be the victor should you try to harm me."

He moved his hand away calmly. "I am not surprised wizard. You were always the meddler, steeped in secrets. They say you cannot be killed by any man now living. Is this true?"

"Who can say?" I replied. "It was not my vision, but Morgan le Fay's that began that rumor." I shrugged. "Perhaps it is true, perhaps not — though you'd be unwise to test it."

Lancelot nodded once, as though this answer somehow satisfied him, but I could not imagine how. "Why did you not call us out?" he asked. "It is treason, both of the hand and the heart to commit adultery with the Queen. Why did you not demand fit punishment?"

He sounded slightly desperate to me, and I felt this a good sign. He was feeling his guilt. "It was not my place to accuse you, but Arthur's. And he chose to forbear doing so for both your sakes, though it broke his heart."

Lancelot hung his head. "You cannot wound me further. You do not accuse me of anything that I myself have not felt in my heart."

I shook my head in bewilderment. Fools in love, I thought to myself. "I couldn't do it because of love," I said, turning to make my way down the hill. "Love is the foundation, the very cornerstone of the world."

Gwynevre quickly dismounted, and she and Lancelot followed me on foot. I could hear them talking softly together for a moment, but I chose not to listen in. Declarations of love, no doubt, and perhaps of regret. Either way, I had not the strength remaining to listen to such things.

As I began winding my way among the bodies, the birds overhead circled lower while the field physicians removed the last of those who might live.

*T*hey caught up to me as I stood over the dragon standard. It was muddy and torn from being trampled underfoot. All around us, the bodies of those who were the last to fall were locked in their grim poses of death. Gwynevre averted her eyes. "What do you here, Merlin?" she asked, softly.

I reached down and picked up the standard. Then I slowly began to fold it. "I am saving something for the future," I said, "bleak as it now is."

She reached out and touched my shoulder. "Please, Merlin," she said.

I whipped around so hard that my long white hair actually swirled cloudlike above my head. My gold eyes were fierce with anger and revulsion. At that moment the thought of her touching me filled me with dismay. "Please?" I said. "Please? That is all you can say? You are the one at fault here. You are the one who was disloyal. And you ask me 'please'?" I said.

Lancelot stepped between us. "No, Merlin, it was not her fault. I am to blame."

I sneered at him. "You are both to blame! If it were not for the distraction you caused with your callous disregard for propriety and honor, Arthur would have been able to withstand Modred's schemes. Now he is dead and the realm with him."

Gwynevre held up her hands. "No, Lancelot, he is right. There is fault in both of us. We are both to blame. I, perhaps, most of all." She lifted her head and turned to me. "But what I did, I did out of love. God help me, it is true. I loved — still love — them both."

I took the folded standard and placed it in a large sack I carried with me. Reaching out, I placed my hand under her chin and tilted her head up as though she were but a child. "Love. It is man's greatest joy, and his most common downfall. Arthur loved you and look what it got him."

"I know," she said. "Still, you must tell us what to do now. Is it too late to fix things?"

I was stunned. "Fix things!" I repeated. "Now you want to fix things? Haven't you done enough? Isn't it enough that because of you, the summerland is no more?"

"I know I wish to make it right, if I can." She bowed her head again.

Lancelot nodded in agreement. "Yes, Merlin. Tell us what you think we should do."

"You wish to fix things, too, great champion?" I asked.

"I do," Lancelot said.

"Then tell her — no, show her, your unspeakable crime."

Lancelot's eyes widened. "I cannot. It would be too much."

Gwynevre looked at him. "What is it he speaks of?" she asked.

"My lady, it is nothing," he said, hurriedly. "Come, let us go away from here. I will take you back to the castle. We can decide what to do from there."

I laughed. "Nothing, he says, it is nothing. Well, what a perspective love has given you, Lancelot. Come now, are you afraid? Is the mighty champion of the Round

Table afraid of the truth?"

Lancelot's breath hissed between his teeth. He was always a man who lived on the outside of his skin, and his anger with me was growing. "No, meddler," he said. "I do not fear. There are some things a lady should not see."

Gwynevre stiffened. "I am still Queen, Lancelot, lest you forget. What is it that you do not wish me to see?"

"Please, my lady. It is nothing, as I said. Let us go," he said, gently taking her arm.

She shook him off. "Merlin, what is this you speak of? Do you now wish to sow dissension among the two of us?"

I smiled. "Not at all, Gwynevre. When have I ever poorly served you? Ever have I been loyal to the crown." I looked at Lancelot. "Will you tell her?"

"Only if I must," he grated.

"You must," I said, "or I will. You speak of making things right. That is a hard road to walk, even when the light shines brightly. Truth will start you on that path."

Lancelot turned back to Gwynevre. "Must you see this, lady? It is not a thing I would wish you to see or know."

She nodded, her eyes bright with curiosity. She had always been curious, I remembered, then realized it was probably that same 'curiosity' that had led her into Lancelot's arms. "Come," she said, "Let us at least be forthright with each other. We've been lying to everyone else for so long, can we no longer even tell each other the truth?"

Lancelot shook his head. "Very well, I will show you. I could not have long kept it from you anyway. Already this thing eats at my heart. But first, I require two things, if I may be so bold."

"What is it?" she asked.

"One, that you hear me out before sitting in judgment on my crime."

"That is only fair," she said. "Besides, with the exception of loving me, you have always been a man of high honor. It is unthinkable that you would commit a crime."

His face burned with shame. "Perhaps once that was true, lady."

Gwynevre raised an eyebrow at this, but did not comment. "And the other?" she asked.

He pointed at me. "I require that Merlin come with us. It is he who cast this stone, and I would have him there to see the end."

"Done," I said. "I wouldn't miss it."

Lancelot set down his shield and pointed towards a cluster of bodies. "That is where we must go," he said, beginning to walk.

"Where do you take us?" Gwynevre asked.

"To Arthur," he said, not looking back.

Gwynevre went white. "But the messenger said his body had not yet been found!"

"I know where he lies," said Lancelot. "Follow me, if you insist on the truth of this matter."

We stepped carefully over the bodies around us, and made our slow way towards the crumpled figures that Lancelot had pointed out. The carrion birds had landed, crows and buzzards, and were beginning to feast. The raucous cries echoed in the slowly gathering dark.

*L*ancelot reached the dead soldiers first, and quickly moved the bodies aside. Just as Gwynevre and I came upon him, he reached the bottom of the pile. "There," he said, pointing. "There is Arthur, my king."

Gwynevre knelt down. Arthur's face was dirty from blood and sweat. His blue eyes were — mercifully — closed. His armor, once burnished and bright, was dented and broken. Lancelot and I were silent. Gwynevre took Arthur's hand and held it to her cheek. "Oh, my bright lord," she whispered. "Would that all had never happened, that I could take this cup from your lips and drink it down, I would." She clasped his hand tightly, and removed his amethyst ring. "For the future," she said. She was crying openly now, her tears washing his hand. I was a little taken aback. In all the years I had known her, I had never seen her display grief so openly. She sobbed, and said, "I am so sorry, my lord." Then she carefully placed his hand across his chest, and started to rise. Suddenly, she stopped. "Lancelot?"

"Yes, my lady?" he asked.

"Where is the sword? Where is Excalibur?"

"I . . ." he said. "I have it." He pulled back his tattered cloak to reveal the hilt of Arthur's sword.

"You?" asked Gwynevre. "Why?"

"I thought to return it," he said.

"Where?"

"To a lake or pond of still water. Often I have heard Arthur speak of how he came by the sword. It seemed right to return it from where it came."

Gwynevre nodded as though this answer pleased her in some small way. Then, she handed the ring to me. "Here. Like the standard, keep this against the future. One day, the darkness may recede." She turned to Lancelot. "This is what you wished to show me?" she asked. "What crime in this? He is dead, as you said."

"Yes, my lady. This is what I wished to show you."

I laughed again. "Oh, come now, Lancelot. You have to tell her. She is no veteran of battle to see the truth in the shadow of how the bodies lay."

"Why, meddler?" Lancelot shouted at me. "She has seen enough I say. Let it be."

"Not enough!" I roared back. "Not by half! Or even half of that! Tell her, champion of honor."

Lancelot's shoulders sagged in defeat — something, I had never expected to see. "I cannot!" Lancelot said, subdued. "It is beyond me." He sat down and lowered his head. In a muffled voice, he said, "You tell her. You seem bent on destroying what light there is left for me, so you do it."

Gwynevre went to him then. "Rest easy. I see no crime here. There is nothing he can say that will take me away from you." She sat down next to him, placing her clean white hand over his. "Speak, Merlin. I am curious as to where your riddle leads."

"Oh, it is no riddle, Gwynevre. But perhaps a picture will do better than words."

"What do you mean?" she asked.

"I mean I shall conjure it for you. Arthur's last moments, exactly as they happened."

She looked dismayed at the prospect, but then shrugged. "If you feel it important, Merlin."

"I do," I replied, and set to work.

Taking up my staff once again, I inscribed a circle upon the soil. Then, I bade Lancelot to find enough wood for the fire. He mumbled something about " . . . not being a damn errand boy," before wandering away to do so. Gwynevre watched me with interest, sitting composedly on the ground nearby. From my back sack I removed those herbs necessary to the conjuring. Lastly, I went to Arthur and removed a lock of his blond hair. By then Lancelot had returned, and was building the fire within the circle I had drawn upon the soil.

Once it was burning nicely, Lancelot stepped away and gestured to me. "Well, wizard, make your magic."

I could tell he was frightened. Lancelot had always had a somewhat unreasonable fear of druids and magic. I chuckled to myself. "Lancelot, I require yet one more thing."

"Oh?" he said. "My blood? You already have my soul, and the heart that moved it. What more could you want?"

"Nothing so exotic as your blood, I assure you," I said. "I merely wish a small sample of your hair."

"What for?" he asked, looking first at me, then the fire suspiciously.

"It will aid me in conjuring the truth of what really happened here today," I said.

Lancelot shrugged. "What choice have I? You have forced the issue and so I must go along." He removed his dagger from its sheath and lopped off a small clipping of his curly black hair. He handed it out to me with some small measure of grace before returning to his seat beside Gwynevre.

"Excellent," I said, turning at once for the fire. I didn't really want to do this, having been through the battle myself. Nor had I any wish to hurt Gwynevre. While she would never have been the choice I would have made for Arthur, he had loved her and in time I had come to appreciate the quality of her mind — if not her heart. Love is often like a battlefield, I thought to myself, filled with small triumphs, joys, and even camaraderie — but there's a great deal of suffering, blood, and usually a few lies to go with it all.

I placed the herbs which I had wrapped around Arthur and Lancelot's hair on the top of the fire. They began to smoke and as they did so, I spoke softly in the language of the druids.

This was the old tongue, rarely heard anymore. It was the language of the fields and the trees. Of green growing things and clouds, of rocks, and dirt, and mice. It was the language of the birds. The incantation rolled off my tongue, and in the cloud of smoke hovering over the fire, a picture began to form. It was the battlefield earlier that day . . .

Arthur is strapping his shield on to his left arm with the help of a squire. He speaks (though it was impossible for us to hear him) to several of his cavalry commanders. He gestures towards the far side of the field where Modred is also organizing his forces. Those gathered nearest him laugh, and Arthur smiles. He glances around one last time as though seeking someone, and then finally he shrugs and mounts his horse . . .

A soldier is making his quick way around the encampment towards Modred's side of the field. Crossing through their picket lines, he goes unnoticed. He is not wearing knightly armor, but rather armor that is old and dented . . .

Modred and Arthur face each other. Modred makes a contemptuous gesture with his spear, and Arthur smiles as though expecting insult. They come at each other, hacking and slashing. It is quickly obvious that Arthur is the more skilled . . .

The soldier is carving a path through the battle. All around there is death, but it does not touch him though he deals it out with quick efficacy. The soldier's blade flashes in the sunlight as he draws closer to where Arthur and Modred continue their fight . . .

Modred's face is marred by cuts, and his helm is dented. There is a look of pain, and animal desperation on his face. He lunges towards Arthur, who turns the lunge gracefully away, forcing Modred's spear out of his hand. It lands some distance away, and Modred draws his sword . . .

The soldier has, for the moment, run out of enemies. At his feet is Modred's spear, and he reaches down to pick it up. He hefts it in his hand, testing the balance of the weapon. A few feet away, Arthur has disarmed Modred again. He begins to close the gap, intent on finishing this combat . . .

The soldier raises the spear to shoulder height and takes careful aim. Arthur's broad back is clearly visible and over it, the face of Modred, seeing his own death. The soldier lets fly with the spear in the same moment that Arthur swings Excalibur at Modred's head. They sword and spear strike their targets . . .

Modred's head rolls into the dust, his eyes wide and staring. Arthur falls to his knees, still clutching Excalibur. Slowly, he drops to his side, forcing his body to turn so that he can see his new attacker . . .

The soldier walks quickly to where Arthur has fallen. Reaching down, he places a booted foot to either side of Arthur's back and pulls the spear out. Arthur screams as the serrated edge severs his spinal cord. His blood is pooling on the ground beneath him . . .

The soldier tosses the spear and it lands in the dirt near Modred's body. He kneels down beside Arthur and removes his helm. As the light fades from Arthur's eyes, an expression of betrayed recognition passes over his face. He dies, and the soldier — Lancelot — takes Excalibur, stands, and walks quickly away . . .

The smoke cleared away on a light breeze as the vision faded. In that span of a few seconds, the only sounds that could be heard were the carrion birds continuing their grisly feast.

Gwynevre leapt to her feet, and turned on Lancelot. "You told me he died fighting Modred. You said they died at the same time!"

Lancelot stared guiltily at her. "I am sorry, my lady."

"Where then lies Modred?" she asked.

I pointed to another mound of nearby bodies. "There, Gwynevre," I said. "There is where Modred fell."

We sat for some time, silent in the near total darkness. Finally, Gwynevre spoke, and her voice had aged. "Merlin, can you give us some light?"

I spoke a word and the crystal at the end of my staff flared. "Better?" I asked.

She shook her head. "Nothing will ever be better again. My lover, whom was once the most honorable man in the kingdom, has killed my husband who was the light of the world. There is no better."

I smiled at her, a little sad. Wisdom, when it comes, is always painful and usually late. "Do not fear, my Queen. We may yet salvage something from this mess."

She looked up at me, and I could see she'd been holding back tears. "How so?" she asked.

"In a moment," I replied, then turned to Lancelot who had remained silent and brooding for some time. "Will you tell her all now?" I asked.

"What choice have I?" he answered. "Now that you've shown this much, what else is there but to confess all?"

"None," I said. "But by telling all, at least she will know the truth. As for the rest, well, we shall see." I must admit it now. I wanted him to suffer then. I knew telling it would bring him pain, but I was angry. His crime, committed for love, was heinous and evil.

Lancelot nodded and shrugged. "Is it your wish, also, to hear this tale, my lady? For I would not do it merely at his bidding."

"Like you, what choice do I have? Until a few moments ago, I believed at least my future with you to be secure. Now, thanks to Merlin, even that is gone."

"Be patient, Gwynevre," I said. "I only do that which

must be done. Do not hold anger in your heart for me."

She sighed. "Just tell it, Lancelot. Let us light this final darkness."

"So be it, my lady. Though the telling brings me no pleasure and I am no bard." Lancelot stood, and walked over to where she had re-seated herself (at some distance from him) on the ground. "This is the way of it then," he said.

"Some time ago, you and I became lovers. That is the bald truth. We had always been friends, but I knew from the moment you came to Camelot that I loved you. Never have I loved or wanted a woman more. Yet you belonged to Arthur, my King. I knew that I could never have you entirely — and I could not find it in my heart to take you from him. I could see the tear in your heart. You loved Arthur, too. Many times, as we lay together in regret, you said as much. We both knew it had to end.

"Yet I still sought some solution. Eventually I hit upon it. What if, I thought to myself, Arthur were to be killed in battle? Who then would be crowned King? Why, most assuredly, the Council would vote for me. As war leader and with Arthur having no heir, I was first in line for the throne. Not that I wanted it, but to have you, and with Arthur out of the way, I would find a way to make it happen.

"But we have lived at peace for so long. Arthur gave us that. Peace and prosperity throughout the realm — his vision of the Kingdom of Summer. But I had heard of a young mercenary of some renown in Ireland. Modred. The travelers said he was gifted in battle, and had many knights among his warband. I sent him a message and asked him if he would be interested in making some amount of fortune for himself here in Britain. He responded with interest, and we arranged a time to meet and make our dark plans.

"I explained to him the situation here, and together we decided upon a solution. For long and long, the rumor had abounded that Arthur was possessed of a bastard son. Modred looked the part almost perfectly with his blond hair and well-muscled body. In fact, he didn't look Irish at all. The plan was simple and direct. Modred would come to Camelot and present himself as Arthur's son, come to claim his due. Arthur, of course, would refuse, and Modred would continue to badger him, eventually forcing a battle. When he came here, Modred had his story in place. He was a gifted actor. He whispered, insinuated, he lied, distracted, and finally forced Arthur into defending his honor.

"But things went wrong. Even before the battle, I saw it clear. Arthur would win unless a miracle should happen." Lancelot stopped and took up one of Gwynevre's hands. "I could not face that, dear heart. I could not see all my fine work to possess you completely, wasted by a fool. It was obvious that Modred had not only misled Arthur, but he had misled me about his battle skills. I was determined to end it for certain.

"I stole some armor and fought on Modred's side of the battle, making my way to where Arthur fought. I killed — again and again! — sword-brothers who I knew. Then, I came to where he and Modred fought. And I killed him. I, Lancelot Du Lac, his champion and his war leader, killed him. It shames me to say it, but it is all truth."

He shook his head and stared out across the ravaged field. "As I said, Arthur killed Modred. Still, his forces were tough, and they fought like wild men. All well-paid mercenaries do. But when our troops saw Arthur fall, all the heart went out of them. Then the standard was lost, and the battle with it."

He looked at her. "I did it for you."

Gwynevre said nothing, only stared at the man she once thought she knew. I felt a brief surge of pity for her, and yet triumph in that Lancelot's character had been truly revealed. Suddenly, she snatched her hand away from him and slapped him with all her strength. His head rocked back, and he raised a hand to his cheek, his eyes flashing. "Go ahead," he said, "it is far less than I deserve."

She sprang at him, hissing like a cat. "You bastard!" she cried. "This was for me?" she asked, pointing wildly around the field. "The warband destroyed? Arthur dead? We agreed to end it!" She slapped him again, and he did not defend himself.

"I love you, and could not bear the thought of life without you next to me. Could not stand the thought of you with Arthur, though I loved him well. I was incensed. I was not thinking of him, or honor, or anything else, but you," he said. "What else could I have done?"

I stepped between them. "Stop!" I shouted. "Stop it this instant! Do you want everyone in all Britain to hear your confessions?"

Gwynevre backed off slightly, as did Lancelot.

"There," I said. "That's better. Now, let's turn to your original question, Gwynevre."

"What question?" she asked, her voice suddenly dull and tired. "I have no questions."

"Ah, but you did," I said. "You wished to know about hope."

"There is none," she replied.

"Yes, there is," I said. "There is justice and bard's tales."

"What have those to do with anything?" she asked. "There is no justice, for if there were Arthur would still be alive. And the bard's have not yet sung this grim tale."

"But they will, my Queen," I said. "Be assured of it. Still, it were better for all if the tale they told was, shall we say, a bit more palatable than the whole truth?"

"What are you saying, Merlin?" said Lancelot.

"I am saying that justice has already been served. And we can see to it that the bard's tales are told in the best manner possible. Your story of Modred and Arthur killing each other, a father and son dying on each other's blades has real possibilities."

"What about justice?" Gwynevre cried. "What justice has been done?"

"Look you here, lady," I said. "Knowing the truth, will you now stay with Lancelot?" I turned quickly to him, and added, "And Lancelot, knowing the guilt that eats at you, will you stay with her and share this poison of your heart?"

"Never!" Gwynevre answered. "He — he betrayed me, Arthur, Britain, and worse still, himself. I could not have him in this way. I will leave Camelot only to enter a convent. Perhaps in serving God, I may yet save my soul."

Lancelot also replied in the negative. "No, I am guilty, as you say. I will leave Britain, never to return. I know what I did was grievously wrong. And I could not be with her for I am poison now."

"There you have it," I said. "Justice is done. The treachery is repaid with exile, and the adulteress with solitude. It is enough."

Lancelot stood. "What happens now?" he asked.

I pointed to the forest. "We will take Arthur's body and bury him there, with all due private ceremony." I looked at Lancelot. "It is only fitting that you should help with this. Then, I will travel the land. The story will be told as Lancelot has started it. That Modred was Arthur's son and they killed one another. Also, I will add a few refinement, so that all hope should not be extinguished in the land."

"Such as?" Lancelot asked curiously.

"That the king was not killed, but only horribly injured. That he will one day return when the land needs him the most. That you, Lancelot, took Excalibur and threw it into the lake where the Lady who gave it to Arthur appeared and took it. I will tell them that she is holding the sword against the day of Arthur's return. In short, we will make it honorable and fittingly tragic."

"That is good," said Lancelot. "It will give the people hope."

"Yes, Merlin," added Gwynevre. "We will do as you have suggested."

Lancelot bent down and with a grunt of effort hoisted Arthur's body onto his shoulders. "Come," he said. "Let us get the worst of it over with before the gawkers come to loot the bodies. Light our way, Merlin," he said as he walked toward the woods.

The three of us walked together, my staff lighting the ground in front of us. It seemed we were in perfect accord, acting in the best interests of the realm. As we entered the forest, we stopped on occasion for Lancelot to rest his tired body. He had a small but painful wound on his hip from the battle, and this — added to the effort of stealing the armor, had taken its toll. Still, Lancelot was a warrior, and his body was strong. We continued on, and made good time.

In the battlefield, the birds had ceased their gluttony, temporarily sated. They now roosted among the dead. At first light, they would start eating again. It would take them some time to pick the bones clean.

I led them deep into the forest, treading along paths known to few humans. Eventually, we came to a hidden glade that I knew of, and Lancelot lowered Arthur's body to the ground with a sigh of relief. I waited for a few minutes, allowing Lancelot to catch his breath. As he did so, I paced the glade and marked an area where we could lay Arthur to rest.

Once recovered, Lancelot said, "So we bury him here, then?"

Noting his cold turn of voice, I replied, "Yes, of course. Unless you'd like to carry him further." I was in no mood to be taunted. We were here to bury the king, and that was in itself a serious matter. I had buried several kings in my long lifetime, but none had been Arthur. Lancelot's statement seemed callous, and I continued, "He was more than your king, boy. He was your friend and your better. Events have proven this true. I would suspect that even you could dredge up some amount of respect."

"Whatever you say, Merlin," Lancelot said, removing his cloak. He knelt down beside Arthur and wrapped the body in it. While he did so, Gwynevre came forward, her eyes shining in the dim pool of moonlight that illuminated the glade.

Kneeling beside him, she cut a small piece of her hair and placed it like a flower in his hand. "For you, my king," she whispered. I must admit to being touched by this. In that space of time, she was singularly beautiful.

Lancelot and I set to work cutting away the sod in square pieces. Once those were removed, we began to dig. With the few implements to hand, the work was slow going, and it would have been impossible to dig extremely deep. While we worked, Gwynevre hovered over Arthur's body. It appeared to me that she prayed.

Perhaps, I thought to myself, she seeks forgiveness from his shade.

We finished the work as the sun began a slow crawl over the horizon. In the forest, the birds began to stir from their sleep. I motioned to Lancelot, and together we lifted Arthur and placed him in the hole. I stood there, looking down on the form of the greatest king to ever sit the throne of Britain. How inappropriate for him, I thought, to be so still. To lie not in state among other kings, but forgotten in the cold ground of the forest. Yet I will remember, and perhaps it is fitting for him. He was not like other kings. I raised my hand in silent benediction, and prayed a swift journey for him.

I turned and saw that Lancelot was leaning against a tree, resting. Gwynevre knelt near the grave, her hands clenched in the folds of her robe. "It is done," I said. "We have but to fill in the soil and return to tell the tale."

"Indeed," said Lancelot, "but there is something I would know."

"What is that?" I asked.

"What is there to keep you silent about this night's work?"

"What do you mean?" I said. "It is for the good of Britain that I do this."

"I've no doubt of that, mighty Merlin," he said. "But you could hold this over us until we die. What favors will you demand over the years to keep silent?"

"Favors?" I asked, incredulous. "When have I ever sought my own fortune? I will demand no favors. I need none."

He remained silent while I continued, "And why should I hold it over you? While it is not easily imagined, even Merlin has loved. I don't pretend to think you have done right, but what you did was done out of love."

Lancelot nodded. "That is true, and all well and good. Yet, I require your assurance of silence."

"I give none," I said, truly vexed. "If my word is not enough for you — when it has always been good enough for the most righteous of men, your king — then all is surely doomed from the start."

"That is where you are wrong, Merlin," he said.

"How so?" I asked.

"Because the only doom here is yours!" Lancelot said, and nodded almost imperceptibly.

I spun around, but was not fast enough to do more than see the dagger — Arthur's dagger! — coming towards me. I was unable to stop it, yet time slowed to a crawl. I watched as Gwynevre plunged it into my chest with all her strength. I felt my mouth gape in surprise and my hand release my staff. Slowly I fell to my knees, plucking feebly at the dagger hilt now sticking out of my breastbone. I could feel myself dying and for one wild moment, it occurred to me that Morgan Le Fay had been right. I had not been killed by any man now living. I looked up at them. "Why?" I asked. "I would've kept faith." My voice bubbled weakly.

"There is no faith," Gwynevre said, "and you saw too much." She shoved me, and I fell backwards into Arthur's grave.

Lancelot sneered down at me. "You were always the fool for love, Merlin. I can trust Gwynevre; her guilt is as great as mine is. But you! You've always been so caught up in honor that there was no reason in the world to trust you." He laughed softly, as he saw the light of realization in my eyes. "That's right, Hawk of Britain. She's a superb actress, don't you think?"

"You . . . you planned all this?" I gasped.

"Most certainly. Though it was last second planning, I admit. I knew you had seen me at the battle. Fortunately enough, I was able to find a messenger and let Gwynevre know that she needed to play along." He turned to her, "That was good work. You did well."

She smiled prettily. "Thank you, beloved." Then, looking down at me, she said. "I am sorry, Merlin. But it had to be this way. I've loved Lancelot for a long time, too long, and Arthur would have been forced to expose us eventually." She looked at Lancelot, who was still grinning down at me, obviously pleased with his handiwork. "It was fortunate that you could send the message on paper and sealed," she said "rather than by word of mouth. All would have been undone otherwise."

"Indeed," he said. He picked up my staff and tossed it into the grave atop my body. I clutched it feebly. I was already feeling lightheaded from blood loss. Lancelot began filling in the grave, starting at my feet. I thrashed uselessly. There was no strength left in my limbs. He talked to Gwynevre while he worked.

"We should get back as quickly as possible. We'll want to start spreading the story immediately. Most likely, there are already people at the battlefield."

"What will we tell them?" she asked.

"The same story from before," he said, then paused looking at me. "But I think I'll use Merlin's suggestions as well."

"How long do you think it will be before we can be together?" she asked. "It seems we've waited forever."

"Soon, I would think," he said, eyeing her lithe form. "Very soon."

Suddenly, she jerked upright. "I just thought of something!" she said.

"What?"

"People will ask about Merlin as well. What should we tell them?"

Lancelot laughed. "I've already got that figured out.

In fact, it's just about perfect. We'll say that at the height of the battle, he was attacked and captured by Modred's mother, Morgan le Fay, in revenge for her son's demise. That she swore she was going to seal him in a crystal cave where he will remain for all eternity, neither alive nor dead." He laughed again and looked down at me. I was barely conscious. "Does that sound 'enchanted' enough for you, old man?"

I was unable to do more than grit my teeth in frustration.

Gwynevre placed her hand on his shoulder. "It is perfect, my love. You should have been a bard."

Lancelot said, "You didn't know, did you?"

"What?" she asked.

"No one ever knew where I was from, except 'across the sea.' I was a bard there, cast out from my people for attempting to seduce the king's daughter. So I fled, and beguiled an elderly knight into training me. Then, having heard of Arthur's court, I came here. To start a new life, and achieve my goals from other directions."

She said, "It makes perfect sense to me now."

It occurred to me then, in the last fading minutes of awareness, that Lancelot had even beguiled her. There was no way she would know it — bards have a magic all their own. I could not warn her. She belonged to him, heart and soul. He had planned this from the very moment he set foot on our shore.

"I think," he continued, "that everything is going to work out just fine. Once all the commotion has died down, you and I will marry and rule Britain. Perhaps we'll visit your father in Ireland after we've taken our vows." He began to finish the grave when I realized I still held my staff.

One last spell, I thought to myself. I began to mutter an old incantation under my breath. Lancelot heard me, recognizing perhaps the quality of the druidic words. Quickly drawing Excalibur from under his cloak, he knelt down at the edge of the grave.

He saw the crystal at the top of my staff flicker. With a smooth motion of his wrist and arm, he brought Excalibur down forcefully onto the glowing orb. It shattered, the pieces slicing into the flesh of my face and neck. I barely felt the pain, was only dimly aware of my final failure.

Lancelot tossed Excalibur into the grave, resuming his task of putting the dirt back in. "There's no way we could keep it," he said to Gwynevre. "It's better that it gets buried here, along with the rest of the past."

She nodded, and I knew she felt nothing for the dead, or for me.

The dirt quickly covered my head. I closed my eyes and dreamed of flight. As the last of the life force left my body, I saw one last vision . . . the winter coming to Britain, and with it, carrion birds by the thousands feeding on the betrayed dead.

Father of Shadow, Son of Light

General Seth Rellick led the vast army of the Kham-Ridhe over a hill and reigned in his mount. In the valley below, the Elven city of Parthanor waited like a shimmering jewel nestled in a Skindancer's navel. The forest of Riantha, which spread over the better part of the Elves kingdom, was not as thick as it could have been — a fact which pleased Seth to no end. It was difficult to fight a mounted campaign in the trees. From here, Seth could see that the gates were closed and the bray of horns sounding the alarm echoed across the remaining distance. Several hours earlier, his scouts had reported that most of the citizenry had either fled or was ensconced in the fortified city.

Not that the fortifications would matter. The outcome of the battle, as far as Seth was concerned, was a foregone conclusion. The advance elements of the Kham-Ridhe, ten thousand foot and five thousand mounted troops, were more than adequate to the task. There were even more soldiers, foreigners and mercenaries who had joined as the campaign wore on, waiting to come in behind his troops.

He raised his right arm, made a fist, and the six primary commanders rode forward. There was no need to discuss the plans, which had been finalized the day before. Seth waited until they were arranged in a semi-circle around him and then pointed at the beautiful city below. Legend had it that the first buildings constructed in Parthanor had been created by ancient gods. "Destroy it," he said. The commanders nodded in unison, and turned their horses at once, barking orders as they rode.

The gods, Seth knew, had surely forsaken the Elves. Otherwise, this war would have been even more difficult. The first ranks of the army began moving down the hillside. Parthanor was fortified, but the gates wouldn't hold for long, and most of what remained of the Elven army had withdrawn to the capital city of Kathas to make their final stand.

One of his personal guard, Marikus, rode forward and inclined his head. "General?" he said.

Seth sighed. "Yes?" he said. Marikus was the leader of his personal guard, but he was not one of the Kham-Ridhe. He was a foreigner and had earned his place by besting all five others of his guard in a single combat. The previous leader, whose name Seth remembered but didn't allow himself to think, had been killed. By rights, Marikus had taken his place, though Seth was still not completely comfortable with the man.

"A messenger has arrived from the main encampment. Your wife has begun true labor, and the child will be born soon," Marikus said. "She requests that you return to the camp."

Seth felt a chill run along his spine. The thought of having a child was exhilarating and disquieting all at the same time — that it should be born as he laid waste to the second finest city in the Elven kingdom seemed an omen . . . but of what? "Very well, Marikus. Send the messenger back. Have him tell her that I'm currently busy trying to overrun Parthanor, but will come or send for her as soon as I'm able." His voice was stern, though not cold, and it held the tenor of command from long practice.

"Yes, General," he said.

Seth noted a slight tone of humor in the other man's voice. "Marikus, try to get hold of yourself. I wasn't trying to be funny. Just have the messenger explain that I'm . . . oh forget it. Don't bother. This battle will be over soon enough."

Marikus nodded. "Will you be going down to the front, sir?" he asked.

The first wings of the Kham-Ridhe were in position. "Yes," Seth said. "Any moment now." On the walls, the Elves were running about, getting their archers into position.

"Sir?" Marikus asked. "We're not waiting for sunrise?"

"That's what they'd expect us to do," Seth said. "So no, we're going to attack now." *Though it appears,* he thought, *that they're trying to get ready as quick as they can.*

"I . . . I had thought everyone was just getting into position."

"They are," Seth said, his eyes taking in the scene before him.

From the trees, six horns sounded the readiness of his troops. Seth turned in his saddle, surveying the strength of the army. The foot soldiers would go in first, drawing the fire of the archers and attempting to gain a foothold on the walls. Their armor would protect them against the arrows for the most part — the

Elves bows did not have a strong enough pull to pierce plate mail. They'd never before encountered an organized army of the strength and resources of his people. Their armor and weapons had been forged by a veritable fleet of Dwarven blacksmiths, taken prisoner when the Kham-Ridhe had first begun their conquest of the continent.

After the foot soldiers took the wall, the mounted troops would sweep in behind them, going through the gate, and leading the charge into the city. Seth and his personal guard would lead the charge against the gate. It was possible, he thought, that they might be able to take the gate — which looked as though it hadn't been used in quite some time, and only recently strengthened with logs — in a single strike.

"What is our role to be in the battle, sir?" Marikus asked.

"The gate," Seth said, donning his helm.

"The gate, sir?"

"The gate," Seth repeated. "Are you ready?"

Marikus waved a hand, and the five other men in his personal guard rode forward. "Yes, sir," Marikus replied.

"Excellent," Seth said. He raised a hand high over his head. "Attack!" he yelled, spurring his horse forward.

They hit the gate and the walls with everything they had, but by the time darkness fell, the desperate citizens of Parthanor, still held the city. Fear of death was a powerful inducement for fighting your best. Seth settled in for a more protracted siege, but it mattered not, he thought as he rolled into his blankets that night for a few hours sleep. Parthanor, like the other cities before it, would fall before the might of the Kham-Ridhe and another piece of the western mass of the continent would be his.

In the distance, the Elven city of Parthanor burned. From his vantage point on top of a steep hill that overlooked the city, Seth could see the glow of the flames spreading into the sky, the black clouds of smoke reaching up like the fingers of the damned to join with the approaching night above. Had it been the city before this one, or the one before that, the sight would have brought him pleasure. The faint echoes in the wind that hinted at the screams of the dying would have brought a grin of victory to his lips. But now...

Seth crossed to the small cook fire he had made and sat down before it. The rabbit was almost done. Behind him, the six knights that made up his personal guard stood in attendant silence, waiting for his commands. Their armor, like his though less ornate, showed gold and red sand dragons on black that seemed to writhe and dance in the flickering light. His thoughts returned to the burning city again, as he turned the spitted rabbit over the flames.

Parthanor was the next to the last. The next city, Kathas, was the Elven capital. There was little doubt in his mind about the outcome of that battle. There weren't enough elves left to defend it. He'd laid waste to their army, cutting it to pieces one battle at a time, though they'd made a valiant stand here. The siege had lasted for over two days. Why then, he wondered, did he feel so restless?

He pulled the rabbit out of the fire, and using a long dagger, removed it from the spit, and placed it on a tin plate. Seth contemplated the horizon glow and his own dissatisfied feelings while he waited for the rabbit to cool. When it was ready, he began eating. The knights behind him were silent, though he knew they were probably hungry by now.

He shrugged, and between bites, said, "Marikus."

Marikus stepped forward, his blonde hair was the color of blood in the firelight. "Yes, General?"

"Go down to the main camp and ask Lianre to come up and bring the child. Get a meal for yourself. When you return with them, send the other men down to eat. You will remain on guard here." He speared another piece of rabbit, put it in his mouth.

"As you command, General." Marikus bowed again, turned and left. His horse made almost no sound on the soft grass of the hill.

Seth finished the rabbit, and threw all the bones except a tiny rib into the fire. He hadn't seen Lianre since the birthing began several days ago, but word had been brought to him that she had fared well through the birth. And that he had a son.

He nibbled absently on the rabbit rib, using it to pick his teeth clean. A son. Lianre had given him an heir. Perhaps that was what he felt — a need to see the boy and take his measure.

Lianre was his third wife, and the only one to bear him a child. The others hadn't conceived, no matter how many times he'd slept with them. It was a damnable thing, and had shaken his confidence, at least in the private chambers of his mind. But finally there was a child.

Seth contemplated the stars again, noted that the fire glow was dimming in the distance. It was almost over. His empire, born of blood and death, the entire western half of the continent, was nearly complete. His urge to conquer it all had led him here.

And now he had son to give it to. But would the son prove worthy?

*L*ianre was sitting outside her tent and nursing her

son when Marikus rode up and dismounted. He bowed perfunctorily from the waist, and said, "The general has asked me to bring you and the boy to him." He paused and when she arched an eyebrow at him, added a belated, "Honored Mistress."

"I am feeding him right now," Lianre said. "I will come as soon as he is finished." She was feeling waspish, and Marikus' half-hearted bow and his tone of feigned diffidence annoyed her. It was the tradition of the Kham-Ridhe people that men should be respectful of women in their actions and in their hearts, but many of Seth's knights were foreigners and only obeyed this only out of necessity. A man accused of treating a woman badly among the Kham-Ridhe risked scorn at the very least. A man found guilty of mistreating a woman risked death.

Marikus bowed again. "I will get a meal for myself and return to you then, Honored Mistress."

Well, Lianre thought, at least he's bright enough to have picked up on my tone. "Very well," she said. "I will be ready." She made a brief shooing gesture, and Marikus strode away, heading in the direction of the cook tent. She sighed. Marikus was an insufferable snob, and he disdained her claim of royal blood.

It was odd for Seth to be summoning her now, she realized. Under normal circumstances, he would be down in the ruined city of Parthanor, watching over the looting and making certain that none of the captives were important persons of rank who could be pressed for information or ransomed. She had last seen him when the birth had started, though she had made certain to send word that all was well and that he had a son.

She looked down at the infant suckling at her breast. The boy was special, she knew, so different from the other children she had seen. He had not cried when he was brought into this world of bright light and loud noises, had not in fact, cried once since. He just stared at her with eyes so blue they were almost black. When he wanted to nurse, his lips and arms stretched outward in a grasping motion that seemed out of place on an infant only a few days old.

But the twin-moon birthmark on his right cheek marked him as much more than just a strangely quiet infant whose awareness was a bit more acute than normal. The birthmark was a part of an old prophecy among the Kham-Ridhe — and she knew the prophecy by heart. It was said that one day a child would come, marked by the twin-moons, and borne under the banners of war, who would cause the Kham-Ridhe to put down their weapons and take up the cause of peace forever.

In the past few days, Lianre had thought of little else, and an odd combination of wonder and worry filled her each time she gazed upon her tiny son. What kind of a man would he grow to be, what a strength he must one day be destined to possess, if he could cause the Kham-Ridhe to become peaceful? She shook her head.

The prophecy, like many of them, was regarded with a mixture of awe and fear by her people. They did not just practice war, it was a part of them, in their blood from the first days of their creation. The Elder Gods had made them that way, and though they were long since gone, the Kham-Ridhe remained.

Lianre was unsure of how Seth would take the sight of his son, destined to be a peace-maker, when the father led an army of thousands. It might well be very difficult for him to accept.

She looked down at the boy, as yet unnamed, who blinked at her sleepily, burped, and fell asleep. She smiled, pleased to have him be happy and content. On the other side of the fire, Marikus was walking towards her and she sighed again, wishing that Seth had sent someone else to escort her.

Nonetheless, it was time to go and show Seth his newborn son. Later, she supposed, there would be plenty of time to think about destiny.

Seth watched as Marikus and Lianre rode into the light from the fire. Wrapped in her arms, and secured against her chest by a clever scarf, was his son. Seth stood up and crossed the small campsite, offering his assistance to Lianre as she dismounted. She nodded her thanks, and once her feet were on the ground, Seth bowed at the waist.

"Lianre," he said, smiling. "I'm pleased that you've come."

"I'm pleased to be here, my husband," she said. Her voice was moonlight and silk, and Seth wondered again why she hadn't pursued more than a passing interest in singing.

Marikus dismounted and tied up both his and Lianre's mounts, then dismissed the other members of the guard to their well-deserved dinner. Without comment, he posted himself on the far side of the fire, distant enough to be out of earshot.

Seth gestured at the fire. "Come and sit with me, Lianre. I want to see my son."

She nodded and he guided her to a comfortable camp chair. "Will this do?" he asked. "Are you comfortable?"

Lianre smiled. "Yes, Seth, I'm comfortable enough." She laughed. "I didn't ever imagine you fussing over me like a mother hen."

He felt himself blush, and was glad of the flickering light that hid his reaction. "I don't mean to fuss," he said. "You probably get more than enough of that from your women."

She nodded. "I did, but I sent them away after the birth."

Seth felt a moment of alarm. For a woman of her rank to be without attendants was unheard of among the Kham-Ridhe. "Why?" he said.

"For fussing over me like a piece of Andari glass art," she said. "They were driving me crazy. I told them to come back after they'd learned to how to behave around a new mother." She arched an eyebrow mischievously. "They may never return," she added in an ominous voice.

Seth tried not to laugh, and failed. "It's just not proper, Lianre. You know that."

"I know," she said. "I'll recall them in a couple of days. I just needed to find my balance."

He nodded. "Very well. I wouldn't presume to understand what you've been through or what you may need at this time." The urge to ask about the child swaddled at her breast was there, but he restrained himself. Tradition dictated the woman present the child to its father, and he believed very strongly in those traditions.

"Of course," she said. "Do you want to see your son?"

As she spoke, Seth saw something — he was unsure what — pass across her face, and he felt another moment of anxiety. He nodded.

Lianre rose from the camp chair. Her black hair swirling almost to her waist. Carefully, she unwrapped the child, then stepped toward him. She held the infant up in both hands, and said the ritual words. "Seth Rellik, General of the Kham-Ridhe and Knight of the First Rank, I present to you the blood of your blood — your son. From the loins of a warrior and a princess, he comes forth, awaiting your blessing and your teaching. From his mother, he shall have nourishment, love, and the comforts of home; from his father, the ways of the Kham-Ridhe, the path of the warrior, the honor of knighthood and a name." She offered the child to him. "What do you name him, Seth Rellick?"

For the space of perhaps ten heartbeats, Seth said nothing. He stared at the little form before him, wondering if all father's saw such perfection in their new born children. Then the child turned its face toward him and Seth saw the intense blue eyes, and the birthmark. He wanted to cry out, to say something that would make what he saw different, but the child's gaze held him, pulled him into its depths, and offered a vision . . .

The banners of the Kham-Ridhe flew over the Elven capital of Kathas. Parts of the city still burned but it was over — the elves were defeated and even now, the last of them were being led to the temporary prison camp. The campaign to take over this part of the continent had been successful.

On the steps of the palace, Seth stood over their King, Thalon, and spoke some silent words. Thalon responded, defiance in his every gesture. With a sweeping gesture, Seth drew his longsword and took Thalon's head . . .

The city of Kathas had been restored. How much time had passed? In the sky above, flights of dragons, black and cruel, were sweeping down on the terrified populace. Archers fired arrow after arrow to no effect. From the south, the enemy rose up in ranks of black-skinned elves, pouring out of caves and underground warrens, to fall upon the citizens of Kathas. Elsewhere on the continent, the last flickers of civilization were being eradicated by this unstoppable force from below the soil . . .

The vision faded, and Seth drew a shuddering breath to speak, but the child's gaze took him again . . .

Seth was leading the Kham-Ridhe across a vast desert. Their armor and swords, the path of knighthood and war, was behind them. Discarded like so much useless baggage. Before them, a harsh realm that could not be conquered, only endured. In time, perhaps, they could learn to thrive here. There would be no choice but to become nomads, moving as the seasons and the shifting sand winds dictated . . .

More time passes, and Seth senses that his bones are long since dust. But the Kham-Ridhe still survive, have thrived in fact. Living in silk tents and raising horses bred to this harsh environment. Their skills as swordsmen have endured, too. Become greater in fact, for the long years of solitary practice. And he can see them, after generations of peace, being the saviors of this world, their swords flashing in the sunlight of a hundred different kingdoms to bring smashing defeat to the black-skinned elves that in another vision conquered the world . . .

Seth drew a long, almost painful breath. His knees felt weak. Lianre was speaking to him.

"Seth? Seth? Are you all right?" Lianre was saying, while she held the child and tried to shake his shoulder at the same time. "Seth?"

Seth shook his head. On the other side of the fire, Marikus sensed a problem and began making his way towards them. Seth held up a hand and shook his head, and Marikus retreated to his original position.

"I'm sorry, Lianre," Seth said. "I . . . I was distracted for a moment. Where were we?"

She looked at him carefully. "You were about to name your son," she said. "Where were you just then? Your eyes were far away from here."

Seth held out his arms. "May I hold him, please?" he asked.

Lianre handed the child over, and Seth saw that the blue eyes had closed and the child was sleeping again. On his face, the tiny birthmark seemed to glow with an inner light for a moment, then faded to a mundane reddish-black.

Seth was unsure of what he'd just seen, just experienced. A vision, yes. But of what? Possible futures? The price of leading the Kham-Ridhe to victory over the elves? He shook his head and sighed, knowing that Lianre was waiting for him to complete the ritual.

The child in his arms frightened him. The prophecy the child represented frightened him. What were the Kham-Ridhe if not warriors born? How could he lay down his sword and lead them off into the desert because of a . . . a child, a story? The very idea shook him to his core. How many of his people had died as he'd led them across the western half of the Astran continent? And how could he turn his back on that conquest now?

Lianre put a hand on his shoulder. "Seth? You must name him."

"I don't know if I can, Lianre," Seth said, whispering. A horrible thought crossed his mind then, that the prophecy had no power over him or his people if the child were dead. He cradled the boy in his arms, arms strong enough to snap a man's neck or throw a spear with enough force to shatter a shield. To kill the child would be nothing, no effort at all.

"You must," Lianre was saying. "He is your son, regardless of the prophecy."

"He will destroy us all," Seth whispered. "We are the Kham-Ridhe. Without war, we will be nothing."

Lianre's eyes narrowed. "Is that how little you value your people?" she asked. "That without the task of killing others, they will blow away on the wind? Is that what you saw?"

"I saw a world I didn't recognize," Seth said. "I am a knight, Lianre. What else could I be?"

"A father," she said. "A teacher, a leader. Perhaps taking the Kham-Ridhe somewhere they've never been before."

"Or somewhere they don't belong," Seth said.

"How long have you wanted a child?" she asked. "How long have you waited for a son to follow you?"

"Many years," Seth said. "But I didn't want this."

"But it's what you have," Lianre said, "want it or not."

"I . . . I don't know what to do, Lianre." Even to himself, his voice sounded weak and unsure, and it brought a twisting feeling to his gut.

"You must do what is right," she said. "Not what you think is right, but what *is* right. The prophecy doesn't say what will happen to the Kham-Ridhe if the child never comes. Perhaps this is because without the child, there will be no Kham-Ridhe. Would you try to trick the universe?"

It was an old question, a philosophy game among his people. It was often jested that every side of a rock, once lifted, was the top side, and the universe would have its way, a force unstoppable.

"This isn't the universe," Seth said. "It's just a child, and an old prophecy. How will I tell the people? How will I explain that we've come so far only to leave the field?"

Lianre nodded. "It will be difficult. They've been following you for a long time, and following the way of war longer still. But they will do as you say, Seth. They will look at the child and see a prophecy fulfilled and the Kham-Ridhe have been following the prophecies since memory began."

For a long moment, Seth said nothing, his head bowed and his eyes fixed on the infant in his arms that would change his world forever. "Very well," he said. "It seems I have little choice when faced with your determination, and the visions given to me by a child without a name." He lifted the boy up in his arms, holding him up toward the stars.

"Blood of my blood, from my loins and your mother's womb, you have come forth. A child of the Kham-Ridhe, waiting to be taught. From your mother, you shall have all the promises of the heart; from me, a sword that will bend and not break, a shield to protect you as you grow into knowledge, and a voice that will teach you of the long tradition of the Kham-Ridhe. I name you Drados, a fire arrow, signaling the coming of a new path."

"It is a worthy name, Seth," Lianre said.

"I can only hope that he becomes a man worthy of it," Seth said. He handed her back the child, who had slept through all the fuss. "Or that we can become worthy of him."

Lianre cradled the sleeping infant to her breast. "What did you see, Seth?" she asked.

"I saw two victories for our people, but only one did not lead to ruin." He shook his head. "It will be hard to tell them of all this."

"They know the prophecy as well as we do. They will believe," she said firmly.

"In time, maybe," Seth said. "For now, we have a long journey ahead of us."

"Will you continue on to Kathas?" she asked. "Defeat the elves as you've intended?"

Seth stared into the fire, seeing the long shadows of war play amongst the flames. "No," he finally said. "We will go east. There to make a new home and new lives for ourselves." He looked out over the hills and thought of all those who had died tonight, and other nights, when the Kham-Ridhe, the Knights of Shadow and Light, had attacked.

"Is there a place for us there?" Lianre asked.

"There will be in time," Seth said. He turned to where Marikus was watching them, his eyes ablaze with interest. From where he was standing, he couldn't have heard much, but must have known something was going on. "Marikus?" he called.

The knight stepped forward. "Yes, General?"

"Recall the unit commanders and arrange for the withdrawal of our troops from Parthanon."

"Sir?" the knight asked.

"We are leaving this place," Seth said. "Never to return in our lifetimes."

"But . . . but General, why? We have them beaten," he said, spluttering. Obviously, the idea of the Kham-Ridhe leaving the field was a bit much for him. "They're beaten, sir."

Seth grinned. "No, Marikus, they're not. Not yet, anyway. And if we do beat them, we'll end up the losers, our people will lose."

Marikus shook his head in disbelief. "What shall I tell them, sir?" he asked.

"Tell them . . ." Seth trailed off for a moment, looking at his wife, and his sleeping child. "Tell them that every shadow can exist only in the light. Tell them that we go to a new place, where the sun warms the ground all year, and the shadows play on the lee of every hill. Tell them that for the Kham-Ridhe, the time to conquer the world has not yet come."

"Sir?" Marikus said.

"You're a good knight, Marikus," Seth said. "Tell them that my son brings with him the prophecy of peace, and we shall find it in the east."

Marikus nodded, and walked away to gather his horse. He climbed aboard, and then said, "General, what did you name him?"

"Drados," Seth said.

Marikus was silent for a moment. "A good name, sir. What shall I tell them to do about the elves?"

Seth grinned again, and felt in himself the release of

all the tensions he had been feeling. He knew now why the destruction of Parthanon was unsatisfying. "Tell them to let them go."

"Free, sir?" Marikus said.

"Free," Seth said. He turned his back on Marikus who rode away to find the commanders and crossed the clearing to sit by his wife and child. Along the way, he unbuckled his swordbelt and set it next to him on the ground.

"We're free," he repeated softly to himself, looking with wonder at the child sleeping, innocent and wise, on his wife's chest. "And we'll never be the same."

Lianre looked up at him. "What's that?" she said.

"Shh," Seth said. "Let Drados sleep. He has a long journey ahead of him."

"As do we all," Lianre whispered. "As do we all."

The Body Clock

The Ghasandi commander stopped outside the portal to the company seer's room. He hated dealing with Malah - the seer, with his bulbous head and pupiless blind eyes that saw far too much - gave him the shivers. Still, he knew it was necessary. The last of his people, 1000 Ghasandi between two ships, were counting on him to make their last hope a reality. He tapped the visitor beacon on the wall. A moment later the door slid open.

"Come in, Commander Darlah, come in," Malah said. "I'm weaving now or I would stand to greet you." His voice was soft and sibilant, a product - perhaps - of his continuous mental distractions.

"Thank you for seeing me, Malah," Darlah said. "I won't take a great deal of your time."

"Time?" Malah asked, and made the peculiar laughing sound of their species: a cross between a hiss and a whisper. "What is time to us?"

Darlah ignored the seer's attempt at humor. "Actually, that's what I came to ask. How soon will we be able to move the fleet beyond the asteroid belt? We've been here some time, and have successfully avoided detection, but . . ." he trailed off.

"But you don't wish to stay any longer than necessary and the cloaking field requires a great deal of energy to support, yes?" asked the seer.

Darlah nodded.

"Your patience has been rewarded, Commander," Malah said. "I have found the human female we seek, healthy and influential, and once we have made the necessary alterations, we can leave. She is called a President."

Darlah's eyes widened. "President?" he asked, stumbling over the unfamiliar word. The Ghasandi had been studying Earth culture for only fourteen solar days, and the most serious difficulty was in grasping the primary language, called English.

Malah grinned. "Indeed, though sorting through the strands took a great deal of time." He held up his four-fingered hands and displayed the intricate pattern of glowing light strands between them. "The population density is very thick on this planet, and finding the right strand," he held up a particularly bright one "and reading it's past, present and future, let alone trying to feel something of the emotions of the person is difficult."

Darlah smiled in return. "Excellent. Where can we acquire her?"

"She will be easily found, Commander. She is currently at a resting place called Camp David. I will feed all the necessary information into your control computer, and you can proceed with your mission immediately."

"Thank you, Seer Malah," he said, giving the seer his title for the first time on this voyage. "You have proven helpful." He stepped towards the door.

"Oh Commander," Malah said. "There is one more thing."

Darlah turned back. "Yes?"

"I know I frighten you," he said, "but I find such emotions distressing to my readings and my weavings. Please try to control yourself better in the future."

Darlah shrugged stoically. What else could he expect dealing with a life-reader?

The landing party, led by Commander Darlah, watched the human woman walk quietly along the path. She was pretty in a stern way, with long brown hair shot through with streaks of gray. It was fortunate, thought Darlah, that the humans were incredibly similar to the Ghasandi, though some differences were evident. Humans were generally taller and possessed four fingers and a thumb on each hand. The Ghasandi had only three fingers and a thumb, with a thin layer of webbing at the base of each.

He turned his attention back to the readout display on his computer pad. Scans of the nearby buildings and grounds showed there to be numerous humans in the area, many of them armed. They are protecting a precious commodity, Darlah reminded himself. He checked the gauges on his faceplate once again, and confirmed that he was still 'invisible'. The light was quickly fading, and Darlah suspected that they'd have to move quickly, before the human went inside one of the buildings and made his job more difficult. He wasn't comfortable with what they needed to do, but knew it was necessary for his people. He motioned to two of his men, and clicked his mouthpiece.

"Get her - quickly and as silent as thought," he said.

Both men nodded and lightly jumped the fence that surrounded the property.

The woman continued walking, shadowed at some

distance by two guards who were listening intently to the transmission in their earpieces. It seemed to Darlah that they were lax in paying attention, though perhaps the pristine surroundings had lulled their vigilance. She was unaware of the telltale shimmer that Darlah could see just over her shoulders. His men were in place, and he signaled the others to be ready. Darlah pulled the wave scrambler from the pouch at his side. The device had been created by Malah and one of the Ghasandi physicians to cause a brief blackout and a memory loss of twenty minutes in humans. He aimed the device at the two guards and fired it. They slumped to the ground, temporarily stunned.

Suddenly, the woman was lifted into the air by one of his invisible soldiers. Her eyes flew open wide, and then shut just as quick when the sleep drug was injected directly into her bloodstream. The soldiers covered her still body in a shroud and activated it, which would make her invisible as well. Both soldiers moved rapidly towards the fence and jumped it again easily, even with the burden of the woman. The entire action had taken less than a minute, and was accomplished in complete silence.

Darlah nodded his congratulations, and said, "All right. Let's get back to the ship."

His squad moved out and the woman slept on, unknowing.

EIGHT MONTHS LATER
*Office of the President of the United States
Washington, D.C.*

Katherine VanStratten looked out the window at the rain falling into the dark street. In the orange glow of the streetlights, it looked like it was raining blood. She shuddered. It wasn't a pretty image, but it seemed appropriate. She turned when someone knocked at the door. "Come in," she said.

Her personal secretary walked in, carrying a tray with a tea pitcher on it. "Good evening, Mrs. President," she said.

Katherine glanced at the clock on her desk. Nearly eleven p.m., she thought. She looked at her secretary sternly. "And good evening to you, Sheila. Why are you still here this late?"

Sheila smiled. "What can I say? You work - I work."

"Just because I'm unable to sleep doesn't mean you shouldn't, Sheila. Why don't you go home?"

Sheila set the tray down and shook her head as she poured. "We're in this together. May as well make the best of it," she said, holding out the steaming mug. "Besides, if anyone needs extra rest it's you. Remember what the doctor said about too much stress."

Katherine took the mug and sipped at it, letting her thoughts drift to the reasons for her continued insomnia. First, she was eight months pregnant - a guarantee of insomnia if there ever was one. She was making history, as it were, by being the first female president in the history of the United States, and the first President to ever be pregnant in office. The elections were six weeks away, another reason for her poor sleep habits, and it was possible that she would be the first President ever to give birth in office. She had enjoyed a fairly successful and popular tenure and the chances for reelection looked good. But there was no doubt that it all of it was stressful. She grinned to herself. She suspected that most of her insomnia during the last few days came from her husband's absence. The "first man," as he had been dubbed by the press, was touring Africa on a public relations junket.

Then a second and far more serious bombshell had hit two days ago. Her National Security Advisor, the Secretary of Defense, and several scientists from the Pentagon came to her with the news that something had been detected approaching Earth from beyond the asteroid belt on the far side of Mars. Speculations ran wild for a time until the first pictures from their long-range telescopes could be analyzed. The conclusion was inevitable: some kind of unknown ships were coming to earth.

All of which caused her sleepless state. She turned to Sheila. "How are we doing on time?"

Sheila looked at her watch. "The latest report from the Pentagon, which came in around nine, said they expect the ships to arrive by noon tomorrow."

Katherine glanced up in surprise. "So fast? I thought they said it would be another week, maybe two."

Sheila pulled the most recent report off the stack on Katherine's desk. "According to this, the ships have apparently sped up."

Katherine nodded. "Wonderful. I'm beginning to wonder what else could possibly go wrong."

Sheila smiled, thinking that the President was actually best in a crisis. "It could be worse. We've contained the news about this. No one outside those people directly involved knows what's happening. We'd have a panic on our hands otherwise."

"That's true. I suppose we'll just have to make the best of it. I'll bet that some amateur astronomer is going to pick this up first thing tomorrow if someone hasn't already." She sighed. "Call a meeting of the Cabinet at nine in tomorrow. Everyone's attendance is mandatory – unless they've got a death certificate, they're not excused." She paused, thinking, then added, "And order a press conference for eleven."

Sheila left to begin making the calls, and Katherine turned back to her contemplation of the rain. Maybe, she thought, it's time for me to drop out of the race. I don't want to be President if it means dealing with issues like this in secrecy. Her left hand absently rubbed her abdomen, which had begun to ache. It was a familiar sensation to her.

More than anything, Katherine wanted this child. Sometimes, over the years, she could have sworn she felt movement down there – some subtle hint, no doubt, that her biological clock was ticking away. Her chances for a child had been rapidly fading, however. She was forty years old, and she and her husband had been trying for a long time.

They both considered it something of a miracle that shortly after their autumn vacation she had turned up pregnant. The media was having a field day, and CNN had been running a "Baby Watch at the White House" segment for the last two months.

She shrugged her shoulders. For the moment at least, she had more pressing things to think about anyway. Like aliens. Fortunately, the baby wasn't due for another month.

Katherine turned back to the stack of reports on her desk, picked up the top one, and began reading. If she was going to be deal with the Cabinet in the morning, she had a great deal of reading to do. Ten minutes later, she was completely engrossed in the material, and never noticed when her hand returned to rubbing her abdomen.

The two ships that were all that remained of the Ghasandi fleet finished their last interplanetary burn, and began the process of slow crawling towards Earth. Not, thought Commander Darlah, that it was really all that slow. By standard Earth reckoning, they'd be there in just under three hours. He could feel his excitement building. For the last eight months, they had waited beyond the asteroid belt. The ship computers kept everything running smoothly, while at the same time, intercepting radio waves and other transmissions from Earth. The information was translated, and the Ghasandi crew spent long hours learning about the people and history of Earth. Everyone now had at least a working knowledge regarding the planet and its inhabitants.

Darlah brought his attention back to the view screen, and called to his communications officer. "Lieutenant Gawpah, what information are we currently intercepting from Earth?"

Gawpah flicked a switch on his console, relaying the translated Earth broadcast to Darlah's chair. "It appears, Commander, that their astronomers have detected our approach.

"Their information dissemination centers, called news stations, are telling of our imminent arrival. They are also saying that the President is meeting in her cabinet and plans to talk to her subjects later today."

Darlah turned on his chair speaker and listened.

"*. . . Again, this is not a hoax, ladies and gentlemen. It has been confirmed that some type of extraterrestrial ship is approaching Earth and will be here in a matter of hours. Their intentions are unknown at this time. The President is meeting with her Cabinet this morning along with several other officials, and is planning a press conference for eleven a.m. this morning.*

"*White House sources have confirmed that that the President has already spoken with numerous foreign leaders throughout the night.*

"*We'll bring you more details as they become available, and the press conference will be broadcast live. Please stay with us as we continue to cover this incredible event . . .*"

Darlah turned off the speaker, and sat quietly for a few moments reviewing the words and inherent meanings in what he had just heard. While he possessed a fair understanding of the English language, he still had some difficulty with subtle meanings, and speech was almost impossible. He reviewed his vocabulary and realized suddenly that the people of Earth were afraid that the Ghasandi might be coming to harm them. He laughed to himself, and his bridge crew looked at him curiously. Everyone on board his vessel were kin-name, and they would understand the situation once he'd made his announcement to the fleet.

He turned on the fleet communications beacon, and said, "Attention, please. This is Commander Darlah. As you know, we will shortly be arriving on Earth, where our last hopes have been placed. In reviewing a recent broadcast, I have realized that the people of Earth fear us, and have understandable, though misplaced concerns about our . . ." he paused, remembering, " . . . intentions towards them.

"It is imperative that we all strive to communicate our peaceful feelings towards them and their society. We are the visitors here, and though we mean no harm, fear can cause events to be misinterpreted. Please remember that the future of our race, of our kin names – the ah, re, qu, lo, and others, resides within our ability to show these people that we wish to peacefully co-exist with them.

"Commander Darlah, out."

Darlah went back to his contemplation of the planet on the screen. He desperately hoped that the people of Earth would come to understand his people. The Ghasandi were a dying race, driven from their home world by a virulent plague that had killed thousands and left those remaining sterile. The journey to this system had taken over two years, and then they had been forced to wait another eight months while the last viable Ghasandi egg had gestated in a human female. Normally, this would not be considered a long time to the Ghasandi, who were long-lived when compared to humans – but desperation, Darlah had come to realize, did strange things to one's sense of time.

The body clock of the Ghasandi, the rhythms of change in aging and maturity, did not closely match those of humans. The normal gestation for a Ghasandi child was about 20 years. But humans aged much faster, and much less time was required. The child would be half-human, half-Ghasandi – something of a risky yet necessary experiment. The biology of humans was close to that of his people, but there were some differences, particularly at the sub-cellular level. The Ghasandi physicians felt, however, that it was possible.

In attempting to create the child, they were hoping to form a bond between the Ghasandi and the humans – a bond shared between mother and child, regardless of its true origin. By their calculations, the child would be born today. Darlah and his people would arrive just in time to help with the delivery of the child.

It was, Darlah thought, cruel to force a child on the

woman without her permission, but the choices of his people were extremely limited. By using the seer, a life-reader, Darlah could find the one woman who would be powerful enough in Earth's chaotic society to shield his people from harm long enough for an understanding to be reached. So, though difficult, he'd made the decision to implant a human woman - the President, as she was called, with a tiny Ghasandi egg. Now, the time of waiting had passed, and the time of action and decision would begin.

He looked again at the planet. It seemed peaceful floating there in space, but he knew it was often a violent world. Still, perhaps his people could bring new hope to them, hope in the form of a child who was both human and Ghasandi - a link between both worlds.

The President entered the conference room looking haggard. They started every meeting the same way, and today was no different. Everyone said, almost at the same time, "Good morning, Mrs. President." It made her crazy when people addressed her that way, but it came with the territory. She seated herself, poured a cup of coffee, and motioned that she was ready. The room quieted.

"O.K. ladies and gentlemen," she said. "It's time to bring everyone up to speed on the situation. We'd thought we had more time, but there's no question that whoever or whatever is out there, will arrive today." She turned to Stuart Warring, her Secretary of Defense. "Stuart, why don't you get us started with an overview and an assessment of what we may be up against."

She barely listened as Stuart reviewed everything that was known to that point. It took almost an hour and a half to cover everything, and Katherine knew she had to finish preparing for the press conference. As Stuart finished, Katherine interrupted before the questions and comments could begin flying.

"Ladies and gentlemen, please hold on for a moment, before we bombard Stuart with questions he can't answer." Everyone stopped talking and looked back to her, so she continued quickly. "I've got a press conference to attend in less than 30 minutes so I can spill this to the American people and hopefully keep them calm. We don't really have time for an extended debate here, and even if we did, I'm not sure I'd want to listen to one.

"I've talked with numerous people about this, including those foreign leaders overseas whose opinions are worth gathering, and here's the way we're going to play it. First, the military is already on alert status, and they're going to remain in that mode. We won't launch anything until we know for sure what's going to happen, but I want them ready to go. Understand, Stuart?" she asked.

"Yes, ma'am," he replied.

"Excellent," she said, continuing. "Second, if they – whoever they are – offers a parley, then we take it. There's no doubt in anyone's mind that from a technology standpoint they've got us beat hands down.

"Third, I'm going to give a press conference of absolute confidence. I'll show the American people that we aren't scared, and are prepared to protect them as needed. But that we're also willing to meet these," she paused, considering her words, "beings as friends if possible.

"Last, I want another meeting with you all this afternoon. I'll be making several announcements at the press conference today, and I'm sure that discussion will be in order. So plan on lunch with me, right back here."

She looked at the people seated around the table, and could tell they were taken aback. Usually, she made decisions after consulting many advisors, and it was unlike her to quickly lay out what she wanted to happen. "Any questions?" she asked.

No one responded, so Katherine nodded and said, "Excellent. I'll see you back here then around twelve thirty or so. Wish me luck," she finished, and strode out of the room.

*T*he pressroom was packed. Photographers, cameramen and reporters milled about in more than the usual chaos. Not a few of them, Katherine thought as she watched from behind the curtains, looked somewhat frightened. She turned to Sheila. "Have you got my notes ready?"

"Yes, Mrs. President. Everything's in order," she replied, then added, "Can I get you some water or anything? If you don't mind my saying so, you look a bit pale."

Katherine smiled. "No, thanks. You're probably right, because I feel pale, almost faint. But, I'll be fine," she said. Then she leaned over to whisper in Sheila's ear. "To tell you the truth, I think it's the baby kicking more than the aliens. With my luck, I'll be a month early and have him right out on stage."

Sheila clapped a hand over her mouth to stifle the giggle. Forcing herself not to laugh loudly, she grinned broadly and nodded. "All right," she said. "But I'm close if you need anything. You know, like an o.b."

Katherine's eyes widened in mock outrage. "Don't say it!" she whispered, "Or you'll set me off." Suddenly both of them were laughing like schoolgirls, and Katherine felt fully relaxed for the first time in weeks. No one said anything, though Katherine caught several looks that seemed to say 'this is no laughing matter'. It made her laugh even harder.

When she managed to get control of herself, she placed her hand over Sheila's and said, "Thanks. You don't know how much I needed that."

"Perfectly fine," Sheila replied. "Though I'll never get used to calling you Mrs. President."

Katherine nodded. She and Sheila had known each other for a long time, since Katherine was just a freshmen legislator in New Mexico. "I don't think I'll ever get used to it either."

At that moment, Katherine could hear her press secretary quieting the room and getting ready to announce her. She turned to Sheila and said, "How do I look?"

"Better than before," Sheila said. "At least there's some color to your cheeks."

"Thanks," Katherine said. "Wish me luck?"

"Always," Sheila said.

The room had gone quiet and the press secretary looked at her in the wings. She nodded in confirmation. "Ladies and gentlemen of the press," he said, "the President of the United States."

Katherine walked out to the podium. For the first time since this whole mess had started, she felt confident and prepared to face the American people. No matter what happened.

Commander Darlah checked his landing crew one last time. According to the transmissions from Earth, the President had just started to give her conference. He wanted to be there as quick as he could, particularly in light of the fact that she was about to go into labor. He looked to his second, Lieutenant Commander Rewah. "Is everything in order?" he asked.

"Yes, sir. The physician is on board, and the rest of our team is accounted for, strapped in, and ready for launch," he replied.

"Excellent. On my signal, Lieutenant."

"Standing by, sir."

Darlah punched in the course setting on the console in front of him. Remembering a child's rhyme from an intercepted television program, he said, "Earth, ready or not, here we come. Lieutenant," he said, "five . . . four . . . three . . . two . . . one . . . release!"

Rewah flicked the release switch and engaged the engines.

The ship traveled cloaked and at a high rate of speed, descending into the atmosphere so quickly that it essentially invisible to the military's tracking devices. As they traveled, Darlah listened to the President speaking. Her voice was strong, he noted, taking comfort in her self-possession. If she could remain this calm in labor, everything would turn out fine.

When they were about fifteen minutes from Washington D.C., Darlah realized from her voice, that something had gone wrong.

Katherine sipped water from the glass on the podium. She was beginning to feel vaguely faint again, but she pressed on. "And so, there is no reason at this point to suspect that these aliens mean us any harm. The military is on full alert status and the American public can be assured that their safety, and indeed the safety of the free world, is our utmost concern." A sudden wave of nausea washed over her, and Katherine felt her brow break out in fine beads of sweat.

It occurred to her, as she struggled for control of herself, that she was beginning labor. Just what I need, she thought to herself. She forced her next words out. "Thank you for your time today, ladies and gentlemen, and now you must excuse me as I'm not feeling so good." Katherine turned for the backstage while the reporters yelled their questions, outraged that she hadn't allowed any of them to be asked. She made a total of three steps before her leg muscles rebelled, and she found herself in the arms of one of her secret service men.

In a moment, Sheila was beside her, holding her hand. "What is it, Katherine?" she asked, forgetting in the excitement to use her title.

The first wave had passed, and Katherine was able to answer. "Just mother nature, dear. Guess I called it right," she said, gesturing to her stomach. "It's time."

Sheila nodded, and in mere minutes, Katherine was bundled up and on her way to Mt. Sinai hospital.

*D*arlah listened intently to the reporter's voice.

"... *and so the American people find themselves stunned in two ways today. First, the confirmation of the existence of life beyond Earth, and now the President is in early labor and will obviously be incapacitated for some time.*

"*She is on her way, at this moment, to Mt. Sinai Hospital, where the birth will take place. What this means, in the face of the oncoming aliens, know one knows. The Vice-President, who has been in almost constant communication with the White House since this crisis started, is on his way back from California, and is expected to arrive within a few hours.*

"*We'll keep you updated as to the President's condition as information becomes available . . .*"

Darlah turned to Gawpah. "Feed the coordinates into the navigation computer. If we hurry, we'll beat her there by several minutes."

The physician on board seemed calm as Darlah looked at him. "The humans are obviously surprised by her labor. Why?"

The physician, Yeulah, nodded. "The normal gestation for a human is approximately nine months. They are concerned because she is starting labor early, though this should not present a problem this far into the gestational cycle."

The ship turned and through the viewport, Darlah could see the roof of the hospital. "Land there," he said to Gawpah, motioning towards the extreme side of the landing pad. "They utilize helicopters for transports here, and that should leave them just enough room if one has to land."

He flicked on the ship communicator as Gawpah brought the ship down. "All right, we're here. Everyone knows the plan. We enter the building and acquire the green clothing appropriate to medical personnel. Anyone we encounter who tries to stop us, must be shot with the wave scrambler Malah and the doctor created. Secrecy is essential until we can speak with the President and explain the situation to her. When the President arrives, we make absolutely certain that we are the ones who treat her. Is that understood?"

His team said, "Yes, sir!" in unison and he nodded.

The ship landed with a light thud, and Darlah led his team onto the roof and into the building. Within a few short minutes, a linen closet on the top floor provided adequate clothing. Darlah listened to the hospital radio transmissions while he quickly changed. They estimated the President would be here in less than five minutes. Darlah assigned two of his men to intercept the President's team of waiting physicians on the fourth floor and to secure the delivery room.

In route to meet the President, Darlah received an all clear signal from his advance team in the President's room. Everything was proceeding according to plan. His team reached the emergency entrance just moments ahead of the President. With the surgical clothes on, no one looked twice as he and his team surrounded the President and rushed her into the elevator.

Katherine focused on her breathing and tried to remain calm. In fact, she'd ordered the driver of her car to slow down several times as they rushed to the hospital. Now that they were here, Katherine asked Sheila to call her husband, as they rode the elevator to the birthing center.

"Already done, Katherine," she said. "Just before we left the White House."

Katherine looked up and noticed that the doctor standing next to her gurney had blue eyes. Her physician had brown eyes. "Where's Dr. Soames?" she asked.

The doctor looked down at her from a chart he was intently studying, and spoke very slowly, as if English was new to him. "He is currently occupied elsewhere. He asked me to care for you until he could arrive." His voice carried an odd accent that she couldn't place.

"Occupied elsewhere?" she asked. "I'm the President of the United States!" she half-cried, realizing as she said it how petulant she sounded.

The doctor nodded. "I know," he said. "I will care for you well."

Katherine looked around in exasperation. "Do you even speak English?" she asked.

The doctor nodded again, and returned to his charts.

The elevator opened and Katherine was wheeled into

the delivery room. Another contraction was coming, and she concentrated on her breathing. When it passed, she realized that Sheila was no longer with her.

"Where's Sheila?" she asked. "She's my alternate coach!"

Another doctor appeared at her side. "All is well, Mrs. President. I will be your 'coach' if it is needed." He turned to the first doctor. "The child is coming soon?" he asked.

"Very quickly," he said. "The contractions are coming faster than I anticipated."

When he said that, all thoughts of Sheila fled Katherine's mind. "Is there something wrong with my baby?" she asked.

"No," said the doctor at her side. He took her hand. "We have everything under control. You should focus on your —" he paused as though searching for a word, "breathing. The child is coming."

Soon, wave after wave of intense contractions washed over Katherine. She lost any thought of Sheila, or her husband. Her face was covered with sweat and her muscles shook with the constant strain. She whispered to the doctor near her, "I can't. I just can't."

"You can," he said, grimly. "You must. This child is the hope of my people."

The words shocked Katherine into full awareness. She looked at his hand, clenched tightly to hers, suddenly noting the differences. Breathing heavily, feeling yet another contraction coming, she asked, "Your people? Who are you?"

The other doctors in the room shrugged, and he nodded. "I am Commander Darlah, of the Ghasandi."

Katherine yelled, barely hearing him, when the contraction hit. "The who?" she asked, desperately trying to make sense of the situation. "You're not a doctor are you?"

He shook his head. "No, I am not. Though he is our physician," he said, pointing to the man seated between her legs, who looked up.

"The child is ready to be born," he said to her. "You must begin pushing."

"Just a minute," Katherine said. "Just a damn minute. Who the hell are you people and where is my doctor?"

"We are," said Darlah, removing his facial covering, "the Ghasandi. The ships orbiting your planet right now are ours."

Katherine fell back in shock. "Yours?" she asked. "Then why are you here?"

Darlah nodded. "Because of the child," he said.

"What about my baby?" Katherine said. "You're not going to take him! I won't let you take him!" She found herself filled with a strange fear, remembering numerous tabloid headlines of alien abductions.

"No, no," he said, trying to calm her. "We have no intention of taking your child. As I said, he is the hope of our people."

The sudden urge to push outweighed any answer she might have given. All her energies and efforts were centered on the child. She pushed, using the last bits of her strength. Her thoughts were jumbled, and she could barely make out what Darlah was saying to the "doctor."

"All is well?" Darlah asked, and Katherine could make out a vague concern in his voice. She couldn't see the doctor shake his head in the negative.

Darlah moved away from her side and knelt near the doctor. They began conferring quietly, while she continued to push.

Giving a last final heave, the doctor exhorting her in his stilted English, Katherine felt the baby leave her body.

"My baby," she said, her voice at a near whisper. "I want to see my baby."

Darlah turned, and Katherine could see he held a small, blanket wrapped bundle. His face looked drawn and tired as he laid it gently on her chest.

"I'm sorry," he mumbled. "He is beyond us."

Katherine moved the blanket aside and looked at the still form. He's dead, she thought, and tears spilled unheeded down her face, mingling with sweat. She clasped one of his tiny hands, and noticed that it was just like Darlah's.

"He is your child?" she asked, broken and confused.

"No," he said, softly. "He is the last child of our race. A plague ruined all our hopes for future children, but we were able to preserve one egg." He looked at the woman, knowing she deserved the whole story. "Eight months ago, we kidnapped you from Camp David, repaired a tiny amount of damage to your uterus which would have prevented you from having children, and implanted the egg. Prior to returning you, we erased your memory of the event. We felt," he paused, knowing how cruel it all sounded, "we felt that this was the only way of guaranteeing our safety until we could discuss the future with your people."

Katherine nodded. In the same position, her people might have done the same. "I understand," she said. "What will you do now?" she asked. Her voice echoed in the quiet room.

Darlah looked at her thoughtfully. "I suspect we will die. There will be no more children for us." Suddenly, he gasped. "Did you do that?"

Katherine said, "What?"

"The blanket moved," he said. "Did you move it?"

Katherine looked down in amazed wonder at the dead child on her breast. "I did nothing," she said. At that moment the child shifted again, inhaled sharply, and began to cry.

As the doctor rushed to examine the baby, cheers sounded throughout the room. Katherine smiled, and this time cried the normal tears of any mother on first seeing her child.

Darlah found himself grinning widely. "What happened?" he asked the doctor.

"The body clock difference!" he shouted excitedly. "The child is half-Ghasandi. Our children are born formless and without a heartbeat, able to grow and gain knowledge at an exponential rate. Human children are different. He's just 'catching up'!" the doctor cried.

Katherine, not understanding a word of the Ghasandi language, knowing only that her baby was alive, said, "What did he say?"

Darlah explained it, being careful to detail the difference between Ghasandi children and human children.

"What do you mean," Katherine said, "that he's 'half-Ghasandi'?"

Darlah looked puzzled. "Of course he is half-Ghasandi. What else could he be?"

"You mean he's half-human?" Katherine asked, holding the child closer as the doctor released him to her care.

"Yes, yes," Darlah said. "He is your son."

Katherine smiled in relief, though tears still streamed down her face. The child nuzzled contentedly at her breast. She held him tightly, as though she would never let him go. "He's mine?" she asked. "My son?"

"Of course," Darlah said, pleased that she was happy to have the child.

"We've got a lot to learn about each other, Commander Darlah. And," she added, "a lot to do."

Darlah grinned at her, sensing that somehow a beginning had been made between his people and hers, the child being only a small part of it. "Yes," he said. "I think we do."

As the rain finally stopped in Washington D.C., Darlah radioed his ship, allowing the President to speak to all the Ghasandi for the first time. She said only two words: "Welcome home."

PART FOUR
Waltzing With the Dead

Waltzing with the Dead

On Sunday mornings, I remember the first girl I
          loved —
red hair so dark it looked like a bonfire.
I cannot escape my own brain.
Mother says I think too damn much, and
I think maybe she's right.

There are days that go by in total loss,
when I'm sure I'm senile, and
can't remember what I had for lunch,
why I'm in a room, or where the light switch is —
sometimes, whole years are gone,
and I wonder when that happened.

And then, for no reason,
I remember a day between 84 and 90.
Parking with Becky on the Platte,
her skin a liquid river under my questing hands,
telling her I love you lies.
We got ticketed for trespassing and the
remainder of the day is lost.

Every day is a dance for me —
a nearly forgotten waltz with yesterday.

I wish I could remember more:
the shape of the birthmark on Brian's cheek,
or the sound of Christine's voice.
Did it look a little like Africa?
Was it the soft ping of rain on a tin porch roof?

I can see them still,
through the twirling fog,
my own version of ghost dancers,
silent, silent, silent
like the sound of ashes falling on concrete,
or the dancing breath of the dead.

Across Hickman's Bridge to Home

The orderly retreat had become a full-scale route, and Boone Coleman was frantically trying to reload and run at the same time when two events happened simultaneously: he was shot in the lower back, and the rammer he was using to pack the powder in his musket punched a hole through the back of his hand.

Ahead of him in the distance, Hickman's Bridge was burning. On each side, Union and Confederate troops peered through the thick smoke of fire and battle to take shots at each other. Boone dropped to his knees in the snow, and pulled the rammer out of his hand, biting back a scream. The first thought that ran through his mind was that he wouldn't be able to work the farm this spring.

Boone knelt in the snow, feeling the strange combination of hot blood on the back of his legs and cold snow on his knees. He toppled onto his side, exhausted and spent. He'd just recovered from a bout of Typhoid Fever, and had only returned to his company two days before this battle.

Boone gingerly ran a hand over his lower back, gasping in shock at the jolt of pain that ran down his legs when he touched the wound. He was just beginning to wonder how to he was going to get the musket ball out when he spotted Mack Puckett through the smoke. He looked around for anyone else nearby, and saw no one — the fighting had moved closer to the bridge as the Union soldiers slowly retreated back across the river. Mack and he were both part of Company H, but there was no love lost between them. Boone thought that Mack was jealous over his reputation as a sharpshooter. *Still,* he thought, *given my options, Mack will do just fine.*

"Mack!" he half-shouted. "Mack! Over here."

Mack Puckett turned and trotted in his direction. "Boone," he said, kneeling beside him. "Looks like you took a couple," he said.

Boone grimaced. "Damn rod punched right through my hand, and some gray-cap over yonder shot me in the back," he said, rolling slightly so Mack could see.

"Not pretty," Mack said. "But we don't have a whole lot of time. Everyone who can walk, crawl, or hop is heading out. The Confederates fired the bridge when they saw us making a run for it, but it'll hold for a while yet. Can you walk?"

"I don't guess I have much of a choice. Might not be a sawbones within miles of here." He lifted his uniform out of the way with a muffled groan. "It's not too deep," he said. "Do you think you can dig the ball out and plug it with something? You gotta, or I'll bleed out before we go 100 yards."

Mack drew his knife, and wiped it on his dirty trouser leg. "Got what I need for both jobs, Boone, but we've gotta move fast. Most of the Company has already moved on." He chewed his tobacco while looking around for other troopers or enemies. Seeing neither, he added, "I'll do what I can, but no more. Sarah's at home with the kids, and I won't die for you."

"I understand," Boone said. "Let's just get it over with. What are you going to use?" Boone asked.

"Chaw of tobacco," Mack said. He worked the piece in his mouth, added a little more, and kept chewing. "This will do her until later," he said, spitting and then wiping a hand over his black mustache.

Boone's eyes widened. "You're going to plug me with tobacco? That's not gonna work for a minute, and it can't be good for it."

Mack knelt down next to Boone, chewing for all he was worth. "How many times you been shot, Boone?"

"Well," Boone said. "This is the first. What's that got to do with it?"

Mack nodded. "So what you're saying is that you don't know whether or not it'll work, right?"

"Ah, to hell with it," Boone said. "Just do whatever you're gonna do so we can get out of here."

Mack didn't say anything else, just stuck the tip of his blade into the bullet hole and started rooting around, while Boone buried his face in his arm and screamed. After a few minutes, Mack suddenly heaved on the knife, and the musket ball fell out on the grass.

Boone was panting heavily by the time Mack packed the chewed tobacco wad into the wound. Eventually, Mack finished his work and wiped his bloody palms in the snow. He also wrapped the hand wound, then replaced his knife in its sheath and looked down at the blonde-haired soldier on the ground.

"You're not much for pain, are you Boone?" Mack asked. "Hell, I took worse than this at Wireman's Shoals and just kept fighting."

Boone gritted his teeth, and spat. "I'll take my share, I guess," he said. "You about done back there?"

Mack nodded. "That should hold it for now," he said. "Can you walk?"

Boone forced himself to his hands and knees, trying to rise. His breath steamed in the air as he struggled, and he made it halfway to his feet before collapsing again. "I can't," Boone said. "I'm just too weak."

"Kinda figured that," Mack said. "Listen here, Boone. The Rebs are gonna be all over this place in no time, and I can't carry you. So what you do is play dead until they're gone, and when the field clears tonight, I'll bring some of the boys back to get you. If I stay, I'm dead for sure. And like I said, I'm not gonna die for you. Just keep still, be quiet, and you'll be fine."

Boone coughed, muffling another groan in his arm. "That shouldn't be too hard," he said, "given the way I feel right now. You'll come back for me though, right Mack?" Boone asked, hating himself for the pleading sound in his voice.

"Sure thing," Mack said. "Probably just after dark. Just lie low, and I'll find you." He turned and began crawling though the still rolling smoke.

"Hey, Mack," Boone said.

Mack stopped. "Yeah?"

"Thanks for the help," he said, meaning it.

"Well, it's better to go to bed supperless than wake up in debt," Mack said. "You'll repay me one day, no doubt."

"I reckon so," Boone said. "But if I don't make it, will you do me a kindness?" When Mack didn't reply, Boone continued, "If you get up towards Johns Creek, will you stop by the homestead and tell Laura?"

Mack was silent for a moment. Then, so quietly Boone could barely hear him, "Yeah, Boone, I'll tell her what she needs to know." He quickly crawled away, and managed to make it within 50 yards of Hickman's Bridge before being shot by a Confederate soldier with either great aim or good luck. *Probably both,* Mack thought as he fell. *I died for that weak bastard anyway.* Then, darkness.

*I*t's *been dark for quite a while now,* Boone thought, *almost two hours.* He groaned softly, but he wasn't really worried about any Confederates finding him. They'd been here for their boys and gone while he alternately slept and waited. *In fact,* thought Boone, *I'd welcome the sight of just about anyone — even if it means being hauled off to prison. Where the hell is Mack? If he doesn't get here soon, I'll probably freeze to death.* His teeth had started to chatter as the temperature dropped, and his legs had stiffened up badly. *I should start crawling,* he thought. *If nothing else, it'll keep me warm and my mind off the pain.*

He stretched out his good arm and pulled himself forward. Pain shot down his legs as his back muscles worked, and his hand ached horribly. He pressed his face into the snow, caught his breath, and pulled again, slowly inching his way forward. Overhead, the stars flickered cold white through the scattered clouds, and the half-moon bathed the field in pale, silver light.

Two hours and maybe fifteen yards later, Boone stopped to rest again. A layer of sweat-ice had formed on his forehead, and his breath came in harsh rasps. He rested his head on his outstretched arm while the heat poured out of him. *Fever's come back,* he thought. *Maybe I'm getting close to the Company. Or Mack will come and find me. Or Laura.*

This thought jolted Boone. *Laura? She's clear over in Johns Creek,* he realized. *I'm sick.* When his breath quieted, Boone heard the sound for the first time. A slow scraping of boots over frozen snow. Boone froze, waiting for the sound again. Silence. Then, the harsh crunch of something breaking through the snow crust. *I've got to find help,* Boone thought. *If it's a gray cap, so be it. I'm gonna die out here anyway.*

"Hello?" Boone called softly. "Is anyone there?"

The sound stopped, then started again. It sounded closer now.

"Hello?" Boone called again. "Mack, is that you?"

There was no reply and Boone felt the first touch of fear. *What if there's no one here? I'll die out here.* He called again, as the sound, the soft crunch of whoever was approaching through the snow, moved closer still. "Who's out there? Can anyone here me?"

A voice, grating and rough, came from just behind Boone. "I hear you, soldier boy. I'm coming for you."

"Who's there," Boone cried, desperate for help.

"Just your old buddy Mack Puckett, Boone. Dead as yesterday's stew meat and ready for you to join me." The voice cackled, and the movement through the snow took on a hectic pace. Crunch, slide, crunch, slide.

"Mack?" Boone said, softly. "I want to go home, Mack." In the silence that followed, Boone's dazed mind suddenly realized that though the crunching sound was coming closer, yes much closer, he couldn't hear the harsh rasp of breathing. When the strong hand closed on his booted leg, Boone screamed in surprise.

"It's me, Boone," Mack's graveyard voice said. "And you're never going home."

Boone thrashed wildly; electric jolts of pain ran up and down his back and legs. Mack — or whatever it was — let go of him, and Boone continued his manic crawl towards Hickman's Bridge. The thing behind him laughed.

"Crawl if you want, Boone. But you'll never cross Hickman's Bridge to home. If I can't go back to Sarah, then you can't go home to Laura."

Boone saved his breath and tried to crawl faster. He was wondering why the Mack-thing didn't grab him again, when the crunch-slide sound started again. *He can't walk either,* Boone thought. *It's a race now. If I can beat him across the bridge, rejoin H Company, I'll get away. They've got to be right on the other side.* He continued dragging himself through the snow, pausing now and again to listen.

Behind him, the sound of the Mack-thing dragging it's broken body through the hard frozen snow continued. It's voice occasionally called out, "Never make it to the bridge, soldier boy." Or, "You're too weak. You're hurt too bad. Hell, I took worse than you at Wireman's Shoals and kept fighting." Or, "I can smell your blood, boy, and I'm so close." Over and over the voice called out, and in Boone's mind it was neither closer nor further away.

Once, during the long crawling race towards home Hickman's Bridge and home, Boone looked up to see Laura standing not ten feet away. He stopped in surprise. "Laura?" he croaked, his voice broken.

The shade pointed, vanished, and Boone turned just in time to see the Mack-thing's hand scrabbling for purchase a few inches away. Boone screamed and rolled, right on top of the wound on his back. The Mack-thing was right beside him — a garish vision of red blood and pale flesh sliding off bones. The uniform was soaked in blood, torn and tattered, and one eye glared whitely in the moonlight.

"Get away, Mack!" Boone screamed. "Just get away and die."

The Mack-thing laughed. "I'm dead already, Boone. And so very cold. Don't you feel it? You're cold, too, aren't you Boone?"

Boone didn't reply, just tried to crawl faster.

Sometime during the long night, Boone's mind began to wander. His body kept making crawling motions, making slow, tortuous progress in the general direction of Hickman's Bridge, but his thoughts were feverish and strange. More than once, he thought he saw Laura ahead of him. Her long brown hair and tan skin glowed in the moonlight. One time, she was wearing a Union soldier's uniform with captain's bars. "Keep moving, Boone. You'll die for sure if you don't get back to your company across the bridge," Laura said. Yet, when he called her name, she vanished.

Occasionally, Boone heard the Mack-thing coming towards him. It was also calling his name, but Boone ignored it in favor of the visions his mind conjured. Another time, Boone saw a young man in a strange uniform that looked like trees and bark. He carried a rifle of some kind that Boone had never seen. "There's a lot of shooting left to be done, Boone," the man said. "And an awful lot of crawling."

"I didn't want to kill anybody," Boone tried to say, but the man disappeared.

Another person, an Indian girl, appeared in front of Boone. "I'll tell your story to the crows, Uncle Boone, and the turtles."

"Why bother?" Boone asked, but the girl was gone.

Suddenly, Boone realized that he had stopped crawling some time ago. The moon was setting, and the sky turning that off-purple and black color it becomes in the hills of Kentucky and Virginia just before sunrise. He looked around for Hickman's Bridge, and saw that it was only a few more yards away. Behind him, the Mack-thing had quieted. *A little further,* thought Boone. *Just across the bridge and I can rest.* He tried to move again, and found that he couldn't. His muscles had locked in the rigor of frozen exhaustion.

Boone tried again, failed, and with a sigh of pain and frustration, cradled his head in his arms. His fingers were blue with the cold, and the nails were torn down to the quick. His back had stopped bleeding, but it ached and sent arrows of pain through his body. Slowly, and without much struggle, Boone Coleman dropped into unconsciousness.

Boone awoke to the Mack-thing's face leering over him. "You were too weak, Boone, and now I've caught you! I'll pull out that chaw of tobacco and suck your blood dry!" The bullet that had killed Mack had plowed right through his spine, leaving his legs useless, but a clawed and decaying hand still had the strength to reach for Boone's throat. "You're never crossing Hickman's Bridge, Boone," the Mack-thing rasped. "You're never going home."

Boone screamed in terror. "NO!! I didn't kill you Mack. It wasn't my fault!" He rolled every which way trying to escape the hands that clutched at him.

"Corporal Coleman!" another voice shouted. "Corporal Coleman, stop it!"

Boone stopped struggling, his vision clearing. The Mack-thing was gone. He was in a field tent, and a doctor was grasping him by the shoulders. "Are you alright now, Corporal?" the medic asked.

Boone sighed in relief. "How'd I get here?"

"They brought you in about two hours ago. One of our sentries found you crawling across the bridge."

"But what happened to Mack?" Boone asked. "He was right behind me, dead and alive, trying to kill me."

The doctor shook his head. "Don't know anything about anyone named Mack," he said. "What do you mean, 'dead and alive'?"

Boone didn't say anything. "I don't know," he finally admitted. "Maybe I was just dreaming."

"Maybe so," said the doctor. "But you're one lucky fella either way. Whoever plugged you up with that tobacco probably saved your life. It certainly kept you from bleeding as much."

"Yeah," Boone said. "I guess so." He paused, and then added, "How bad am I hurt?"

"Not as bad as could be," he said. "But you'll be on leave for awhile before you see any action again." He straightened Boone's blankets and looked around the tent. "I've got others to see," he said, "But I'll come back and check on you in awhile. You need to rest now."

"Ok," said Boone.

The doctor walked away, and Boone slept again.

*T*he North had driven the Confederate soldiers back again, and when he was able, Boone searched the field on the other side of Hickman's Bridge for Mack's body before heading for home. His uniform was found in tatters near the bridge where he fell. *They must've found his body,* Boone thought. *It was nothing but a dream that scared me into saving my own life. Mack's dead, and it's over.*

It took several days for Boone to reach his homestead on Johns Creek. On the way, he passed within a mile of Bradshaw, where Mack Puckett had lived with his wife Sarah. He wanted to stop and pay his respects, but decided to continue on to home. He wanted to hold Laura in his arms and see his how his land had fared in his absence.

An hour later, Boone rounded the bend in the road leading to the red and white painted farmhouse. Smoke curled up from the stone chimney, and he could almost smell the dinner Laura would cook for him that evening. He reined in his horse in the yard, and hitched it to the post next to an ugly, grayish horse already there. *I don't remember owning that nasty looking beast,* Boone thought. *Maybe there's a visitor come calling.*

The door opened and Boone saw Laura standing there, half in shadow, half in sunlight. "Laura," he said, softly. "I'm home."

She didn't speak, just crossed the old porch in three quick strides and threw herself into his arms. "Boone!" she whispered, nearly sobbing. "You're alive! You're alive!" Her face was buried in his neck, and he could smell the soap and spring water in her hair.

He turned her face up towards his and kissed her soundly. "Last I checked, woman," he said, smiling. "Though not without a scar or two."

"Oh, Boone!" she said. "That ugly man inside said you were dead. Killed on the field just past Hickman's Bridge. He said he was there."

"There's a mistake made somewhere, Laura," Boone said. "Let's go in and meet this fellow. I want to know who counted me dead before I even left the camp."

Arm in arm, they strode into the house together. The smells of home surrounded Boone — vegetables and meat cooking on the fire, fresh sawdust on the floor.

"Oh, you already know him," Laura continued. "You remember Mack Puckett, right?"

Boone stopped in surprise as the Mack-thing stood to great him. "Hello, Boone," it rasped, smiling its graveyard smile. "You may have won the race to Hickman's Bridge, but I still beat you home."

Boone stared as the Mack-thing came closer, somehow healed of its horrible injuries, somehow looking all the worse for the multitude of scars running over his face. It now wore a tattered officers uniform, but the Mack-thing was changing even as it approached. He stared as the Mack-thing came closer, and Laura tugged at his sleeve, begging him to tell her what was wrong. When she saw the horrible changes in the Mack-thing, the rotting hair and flesh, the open wound, the whitely staring eyes, she screamed once and fainted.

The Mack-thing's hand closed around Boone's wrist; a grip so cold and firm that Boone knew there was no escape this time. "You're a dream," Boone whispered. "Just a dream."

The Mack-thing laughed, and Boone could smell sulfur and brackish water. "No dream, soldier boy. This is no dream at all."

Boone found the breath to scream one last time as the Mack-thing lunged towards him, keeping his battlefield promise to come back for him.

The sounds from the Boone farmstead echoed over the darkening hills, but no one heard them, not even Sarah Puckett, who tucked her children into bed, turned down the lights, and prayed that the soldiers who informed her of Mack's death were wrong. That he was still out there somewhere, still alive, and that he would come home.

AUTHOR'S NOTE

Sometime around 1994, my grandmother gave me a document written by an extremely distant relative named Brian Patrick Hembling that details a part of our family history during the Civil War. Written, I gather, due to a fascination with both the Civil War and our family's rather convoluted history, it tells the story of the Daniel Boone Coleman family and the Malachi Puckett family (both distantly related to yours truly). I haven't, unfortunately, been able to find Brian Patrick Hembling, but in reading his document, the ideas for this story occurred. I have taken numerous and excessive liberty's with the facts of the stories, and the tale is in no way a reflection of the true events at Hickman's Bridge in Kentucky. And by the way, if you happen to see Brian, let him know I said thank you.

Dead Tired

The first time Jack Morris died in his sleep was just before two a.m. during a particularly hot July morning. He knew the time because the digital clock was the first thing he saw after rising to his knees from the floor where he had landed. He unwound the sheets from his legs and brushed a shaking hand across his forehead. Jack could feel cold, clammy sweat running in small rivulets down his neck and back.

He laughed in relief. "No wonder\ you're sweating, you dipshit," Jack said to himself, "Just be thankful you're alive." But sixty seconds ago he hadn't been, or at least he hadn't thought so. The dream had been nothing short of terrifying, In it, Jack had been running from an unseen assailant who screeched in fury and malevolent glee at his hapless victim. The sound had reminded Jack of train brakes — a high-pitched squeal of metal on metal. Every time he tried to face his opponent, invisible fists had pounded him in the face, the stomach, even his crotch. Finally, exhausted and bloodied, Jack had found himself cornered in an alley. The walls were slick sheet metal and glowed with a faint light, He turned to fight one last time and saw the light glint off a knife blade.

The attacker spoke softly, hardly winded at all compared to Jack's labored breathing. The voice was low and husky, but somehow, Jack thought, vaguely familiar. Yet he couldn't place it, nor could he see his attacker as he spoke. "This is for all of us, you bastard." Then the knife swooped down in a sudden arcing motion, and Jack screamed like a girl as his balls dropped with a wet, red splat to the pavement. The knife arced once more and buried itself in his throat. In the dream, Jack knew he was dead, long agonizing seconds before his battered body dropped to the ground.

Sitting on the floor beside his bed, Jack shook his head in stunned amazement. He'd always had very real dreams, but he suspected he wouldn't be forgetting this one for quite some time. Jack also realized that his whole body ached, as though he'd actually been running and fighting his opponent. He slowly stood up and tossed the sheets and blankets back on the bed. He felt stiff and sore all over. "Must've really been thrashing around," Jack mumbled to himself. He turned and walked to the bathroom.

As he reached blindly for the switch, Jack considered taking a quick shower. Aside from being sore, his whole body was alternately slick and sticky from sweat. The light came on with ruthless brilliance and Jack stumbled toward the toilet. Suddenly, he caught a glimpse of himself in the mirror and stopped cold. Taking in what he saw caused his whole body to break out in gooseflesh. For the second time that night, though he thought it was the first, Jack screamed out loud.

In the mirror, Jack saw his disheveled brown hair dangling limply from his scalp. His eyes were hung with bags which were almost black. His left eye was beginning to swell with a bruise, and there were other bruises and marks all over his body. But it was not any of that that made him scream. It was the thin trickle of blood running from the cut on his throat, and the similar stream which was winding its way down his right thigh. Completely awake, Jack thought he really had been stabbed. During that first second or two, he could almost imagine the wicked knife protruding from his throat.

"Jesus," he said. Looking more closely, Jack saw that in actuality, the wounds were nothing more than scratches. Just deep enough to draw a little blood. He remembered hearing about this type of thing. In a dream, a person would think something was happening to them, and somehow, usually without even knowing it, the person would make a similar injury on his own body. As he had. He'd obviously just scratched himself during the dream. Based on the number of bruises and welts, he'd done a really good job. Still, it was damn creepy seeing yourself in the mirror like that with no one else around to blame for the damage.

Jack urinated and showered. The blood and sweat disappeared, but of course, the bruises and other marks stayed. As he lay back down to try and get some sleep, Jack remembered something else he'd heard about violent dreams. If you died in your dreams, he recalled, then you were supposed to die for real. Like if you fell off a cliff, you were okay unless you hit the ground. If that happened, supposedly you'd have a heart attack and die for real.

Lying there, Jack thought that it must be a goofy superstition or something. He'd "died" in his dream, and aside from the damage he'd done to himself, he felt fine. He turned over and for the rest of the night, Jack Morris slept like a baby.

That morning, Jack got up and dressed. He had his coffee and bagel and waited for his neighbor, whom he carpooled with, to pull up and honk. At twelve minutes after eight, he did. Jack walked outside to the car and got in. "Morning, Rob," Jack said as he shut the door.

"Morning, Jack," Rob replied as he put the car in reverse. That was when he saw Jack's eye and hit the brakes. He looked his friend over a little more closely. "What the hell happened to you? You and Sue weren't fighting again, were you?"

Jack laughed. "Hell, no! She's staying with her mother until we get things worked out."

Rob raised an eyebrow. "Oh, yeah? Well, then what the hell was all that yelling coming from your place last night? You listening to heavy metal now?"

Jack flushed. "No, no. It's nothing like that, or what you're thinking. I had a nasty nightmare — I know it sounds silly — and hollered a little, I guess."

"Must've been some nightmare to give you a shiner like that." Rob sounded unconvinced.

"Yeah, well, I think maybe I actually beat myself up a bit while I was dreaming. Scared the shit out of me really. Trust me Rob, Sue is fine."

Rob shrugged. "Okay, man. If you say so. I just don't want to be bailing your ass out of the joint again for beating on your wife, know what I mean?"

Jack nodded. "Yeah, I know exactly what you mean. C'mon, let's get to work."

"All right," said Rob.

On the freeway, they didn't talk much. This left Jack free to think about the time that Rob had bailed him out of jail. It had been an ugly incident. Jack and Sue had been married for only six months the first time he hit her, and during the next seven years, the pattern had gradually gotten worse. Rob didn't know that much about Jack, especially about his childhood.

As a boy, Jack's father, Tom, had been the same way

toward him and his mother. If dinner wasn't ready on time, or his clothes weren't pressed just right, Jack's father would "give her a little discipline." Usually by beating the shit out of her. Jack wasn't immune either. The end of all that came the year Jack was twelve. His father had been badgering him all spring to try out for Little League, and Jack had finally agreed. Then they were in the backyard, with Jack's father trying to teach his son how to hit a baseball.

Jack tried, he really did. But the harder he swung, the more he missed. First, his father started badgering him verbally. "Come on, boy. Let me see you actually hit one! You swing like a girl. Is that what you are? A little girly girl?" Jack tried harder and failed. Tom Morris, a big man at just over six feet, two inches tall, began to get angry. "Well, Jackie," he always called him that, "I guess you just need a little discipline. I guess I'm gonna have to teach you how to hit that ball like a man."

At first, he just said this and kept pitching. With each throw, however, Tom Morris threw the pitch a little harder and a little faster. Under his breath, Jack could hear him mumble, "Hit the ball, gonna teach you how to hit the ball." Eventually, the inevitable happened. A very hard pitch went the wrong way and Jackie missed the ball. As might be expected, however, the ball didn't miss him. It struck him squarely on the collarbone, breaking it with a dry *snap!* that sounded like a brittle stick being stepped on. Jackie screamed and dropped the bat, while an angry Tom Morris stood over his son.

"Well isn't that typical. You're just a damn sissy. You get hit with a little fast ball and you cry like a baby. You sure you're a boy?" Tom spoke faster and faster, spittle flying from his lips. "Jackie, I'm gonna show you how to use this bat. I'm gonna show you how to hit the ball." Tom picked up the bat and swung it lightly in his hands. "Here we go, Jackie. Pay attention now, 'cuz I'm gonna show you how to hit that ball." With every repetition of the word ball, Tom slapped the bat into his opposite palm.

In a moment, he seemed to go crazy. "Hit the ball, Jackie! Hit the ball!" All the while he screamed this, he hit his twelve-year-old son with the bat. Jack was lucky to have survived. The scene was spotted by the neighbors who called the police. Tom Morris skipped bond and was never heard from again. And little Jackie Morris healed, grew up, and vowed to never be like his dad. But patterns repeat themselves, and at twelve, that pattern had already been well established in Jack Morris' mind.

During his marriage to Sue, Jack had been unable to control himself. Little things she did or didn't do seemed to enrage him for no real reason. He began to "give her a little discipline" to the point that the last time — the time Rob had bailed him out — he'd put her in the hospital. They had talked a few times since — on the phone, only — but Jack thought that maybe with work they could put things back together. He wanted to, and promised to try. Jack wasn't going to run away like his father had. The only fortunate thing was that he and Sue didn't have children yet. They'd been trying off and on for a couple of years, but nothing had ever come of it. In the calm after the storm, Jack realized that maybe it was because she'd miscarried more than once.

Rob was saying something.

"What's that?" Jack asked.

"I was saying that you really must be sleep deprived because for a minute there, you were off in never-never land, What were you thinking about'?"

Jack shrugged. "Sorry, Rob. Just thinking about baseball." A few minutes later, Rob parked the car, and Jack went to work.

That night, Jack spoke to Sue again. The heat must have made them both a little testy. The conversation was short and curt. Before a full-fledged argument could break out, Sue suggested that the call end. Jack had agreed. He ate his TV dinner and watched the news before going to bed. When the dream came, Jack moaned softly in his sleep.

The alley was the same, the light dim and red, his pursuer the same shadowy form. Jack tried to run, tried to find an argument that would appeal to his attacker, but nothing could stop him. As before, Jack found himself battered and bleeding and cornered. This time, the illuminated weapon was a bat. An old and dented aluminum one. Jack could see spots of blood on it. He strained to see in the dim light. "Why?" he asked, though somehow he knew it was senseless, a dream phantom.

The thing, Jack was sure it was a thing now, giggled. And to Jack it sounded like the laugh of an evil child. "Because you learned to hit the ball, Jackie. You learned to hit the ball!" The bat swung with deadly force and accuracy. Before the lights went out completely, Jack saw his brains dripping off the end of the bat. His hair was matted on it.

When Jack awoke on the floor, he didn't move. He lay still and puzzled out that because he'd been thinking of that last incident with his father, the thing used a bat this time. *It didn't matter,* he told himself, *it was only a dream.*

He staggered into the bathroom. The damage was worse this time. Blood ran freely from his ears and nose as though he'd been repeatedly beaten. His eyes were puffy and blackened. Jack laughed weakly while he washed himself up. Occasionally, he cried. He talked to himself in low tones. "I'm beating myself up in my dreams, that's all. That's all it is. I just gotta get control of myself, stop getting so worked up. It's just a dream."

By the time he crawled back into bed, Jack had almost convinced himself, When the alarm clock sounded, he shut it off and immediately reached for the phone. Spots of light swam before his eyes when he moved. Rob answered, still using his just-got-out-bed voice. "Yeah."

"Rob, it's Jack." His voice was almost a croak.

"What is it, Jack?"

"I can't go in to work today. I'm not feeling so hot."

"No wonder, with all the yelling you were doing last night."

"What yelling?"

"Good Christ, Jack. You were screaming and carrying on for nearly thirty minutes."

Thirty minutes? Jack was positive the dream had lasted hours. "You're kidding!"

"Shit, no! But I could also see that there were no lights on and that Sue's car wasn't in the drive. Were you dreaming again?"

"Yeah, something like that, Can you cover for me today?"

Rob sighed. "Yeah, no problem." He paused. "Maybe you oughta get some help or something. You didn't beat yourself up again, did you'?"

Jack forced a laugh. "Naw, I'm just feeling a little wrung out, you know. I haven't been sleeping all that great."

"Okay, man, if you say so. Listen, I'll see you tomorrow, right?"

"You betcha," Jack said. "Later."

"Later, " Rob said, and hung up.

Jack lay back down with a sigh. If Rob saw him all beat up like this, he'd think something was going on for sure. Better to lie low for a couple of days. Jack spent the day lounging and watching television. He moved slowly and with great care. His entire body was bruised, and if he walked too fast, he got dizzy. He didn't sleep, nor did he call Sue. *Shit,* he thought, *she'd never believe it anyway.* He wasn't sure if he did. The entire thing seemed unreal. That night, the dream repeated itself, but for a few things.

This time the weapon was a broom handle wrapped in wire. And Jack could almost see his attacker. The thing which writhed underneath a dark shroud of some type was almost visible. When Jack was cornered, he again pleaded with it to tell him why. It giggled again, still reminding Jack of a child, and then it said one word.

"Revenge."

Jack awoke, more battered than on any previous night. He was bleeding in several places and had to crawl to the bathroom. It occurred to him that this dream might just kill him.

In the morning, he called Rob again and begged off for the rest of the week. He explained that he'd decided to take a mini-vacation, he had the time coming, to do some serious thinking, He wanted to get things settled with Sue. Rob seemed pleased.

"Hey, that's great, man. I didn't hear any screaming last night either. How'd you sleep?"

"Fine," Jack lied, "just fine." He didn't bother to tell Rob that he couldn't have screamed because his face was buried in a pillow, and his throat was half-filled with blood.

Jack signed off. That night, he drank coffee until four a.m. and didn't sleep at all.

Jack managed to stave off sleep for three days. He barely ate, and when he did, the food tasted like ash in his dry mouth. On the fourth night, Jack couldn't take it anymore. He staggered into his bedroom and collapsed into sleep. Within an hour, Jack Morris was dreaming again.

This time was no different. The thing beat him, chased him, and beat him some more. No weapon was needed. Jack could barely walk, let alone run. Jack knew he was dreaming, yet was helpless to stop it. He knew he was dying, and there was no reasoning with the strange creature that was destroying him. When he found himself cornered one last time, Jack turned and said, "At least let me see you!" He was crying in fear and frustration and pain.

The creature stopped and seemed to look right at him. It was just visible in outline. It giggled. "You don't recognize me?"

Jack sobbed. "No, damn it! No!"

"You should," the thing said. It removed the shroud that covered its body, though it still wasn't visible. "We're a part of each other. "

"What do you mean? "

"I mean *I'm* a part of *you*, Daddy!" And the creature stepped into the light. Jack Morris wanted to scream and couldn't. All his breath was gone. The thing was a strange mix of children's body parts. They were wet and bloody and twisted madly about themselves like snakes in a nest.

The creature, Jack suddenly realized in horror, was all the children he had ever created with Sue. They were miscarriages, and they spoke with one voice he could easily place now. His own. Guilt and fear swept over his body, and as his children fell on him in a crushing embrace, Jack Morris found the strength to scream one last time.

On Monday morning, Rob broke down the door to Jack's house and found his friend's battered body on the bed. Blood had pooled and stagnated in the sheets. There were even splashes of it on the walls. Rob thought he'd be okay until he realized that Jack was trying to speak. He could barely manage a whisper.

Rob quickly knelt beside him. "What is it, Jack? What happened?"

Jack shuddered. "My children, I killed my children. Then they killed me." And with that, Jack Morris died.

Rob looked at the carnage around the room and was violently sick. Then he called the police.

A week later they were calling it a "ritual homicide." They had no suspects. Rob helped Sue through the ordeal as best as he could. Life went on.

As might be expected, Rob and Sue eventually married. They even had children. Rob never mentioned what Jack had said. He assumed that Jack had been delusional. Both Rob and Sue slept well at night, and the children did, too.

A Kiss at Midnight

for Misti

"On Sunday mornings I remember the first girl I loved,
red hair so dark it looked like a bonfire."
— From *Waltzing With the Dead*

> Very attractive, SWF in search of passionate SWM for one night stand.
> Must understand the hungers of the flesh. Guaranteed unforgettable evening. Discretion a must. Send picture and bio to Box 8267–473.

I imagine her this way:
She wakes to red velvet and lace. Though there is not the tiniest sliver of light in the darkness, her green eyes can make out the tiny swirls in the fabric of the cloth canopy above her with ease. She licks her dry, red lips, and her delicate, pale hands move over the white silk sheets of her bed. She rises, her long, red hair a pillow-cloud around her shoulders, and she greets the night once again — a beautiful angel of love and lust and

death. She wakes in this manner every night, as she has every night before . . .

I fell in love with her in a single night. I answered her ad, expecting nothing more than an evening of enjoyable, commitment-free sex. I didn't get what I expected — nor, I suppose, did she. For long months, I have been thinking only of her. Trying to find her once again so I can tell her that now I understand that true love does not care about the murky boundary waters between life and death, good and evil, or right and wrong. Love is the desire to consume oneself in the flames of another person — the flesh, minds, and souls combine and grow into a fire that burns with starlike heat at its most passionate, or burns out into the cold oblivion of darkness when it fails . . .

I started browsing the personals a year after my wife, Anaka, was killed in a car accident. At first, I found them grimly amusing — the desperate acts of people who were unwilling or unable to meet others in the real world. I didn't realize then how desperate I myself would become; when the long days at work would become longer nights at home, sitting in a silence that no music or television program could breach. I became a recluse of sorts. I didn't go out, didn't meet people, and didn't start my life over as I'd planned when the shock and grief of losing my wife had passed. I was alone, and reading the personals — at first a joke to me — became a quest to connect somehow with someone else, to live again.

I was scared, of course. Who wouldn't be in this age of unreason? I read the ads in the paper, over and over, searching for the ones that would interest me enough to answer. I had a process of reading them in no time at all — ignore every ad that involved men, couples, or home videos, and read every ad that involved a single female. It shortened the list considerably.

Occasionally, I would find the courage to respond to an ad, only to find that the people who placed the ad had misrepresented themselves. The women would — in actuality — be men, or unattractive to me, or simply undesirable in some other fashion. I went on several unsuccessful first dates before I decided to approach it from the other direction.

The day finally came when I placed my own ad, to generally poor results. Usually it read something like:

> SWM, 30-something, not hard on the eyes, seeking SWF for relationship, possible long-term commitment. He is secure, honest, and intelligent. She must demonstrate similar qualities. Reply to Box 9673–626.

More often than not, a brief phone conversation ended any hope of meeting in person — the results from this direction were the same as they were from the other one. It didn't seem to matter whether I was the advertiser or the respondent, everyone seemed unreal to what they said they were. After one such phone call, I realized that I was being too particular. I also realized that I didn't really care. I was looking for someone who could replace my wife, my soul mate — and that didn't seem possible anymore. How do you go about replacing someone who is irreplaceable? I didn't want to risk love anymore, or face the pain of losing a loved one.

At night, I would lie awake and remember Anaka in vivid detail. The way her dark hair curled when it was wet, the color of her eyes in candlelight, the sound of her voice, husky and low after we'd made love. I didn't believe that anyone could measure up to her. The very idea of love began to seem a little sad to me, like finding out that your religion is based on a falsehood.

Yet there was no doubt in my mind that I still longed for the touch of a woman. I became more and more lonely, and as the days and nights passed, I found that almost more than anything else, I missed physical intimacy. I would walk along the pier, fascinated by the way a woman's hips looked inside her jeans, or the press of her breasts against the fabric of her shirt. The scent of women's perfume mixing with the smell of the ocean in an intoxicating blend, the fading light of the day turning faces and forms into silhouettes that could — in my minds eye — be a replacement for my lost Anaka.

Finally, I decided to ignore my continuing quest for true love, and find a way to appease my physical desires. Perhaps by extinguishing my lust I could find a path back to a place where love was possible again. I felt my desires were perfectly normal, and at the very least I would be on the same page as the other lost souls who were investing their time in the personals. My temporary hold on finding true love again would, if nothing else, save me from continued disappointments.

And then I saw her ad for the first time:

> Very attractive, SWF in search of passionate SWM for one night stand.
> Must understand the hungers of the flesh. Guaranteed unforgettable evening.
> Discretion a must. Send picture and bio to Box 8267–473.

The hungers of the flesh. I liked the sound of that a great deal. That is what I was suffering from . . . a hunger for the touch of flesh. How I lusted for the sweet scent of a woman's skin, the taste of her lips on mine. I sent her my picture, and a one-page description of myself and my life — such as it was. And I waited, in a strange state of trepidation and excitement, hoping for the phone to ring.

*T*he call came an hour after sundown.

"Hello?" I asked.

"Good evening," the low voiced, female caller said, "Is this Jameson Servais?"

My heart pounded. Was it her? Telemarketers never pronounce my name correctly, and I had mentioned the correct pronunciation in my letter to her. I swallowed hard, and my tongue clicked once, dryly.

"Hello?" she said. "Are you there?"

"Yes," I managed to croak. "This is Jameson."

"Hello," she said. "You answered my ad."

"I guess I did," I said, feeling nervous.

"I'm glad," she said. "I was impressed."

"Well, uh, then I guess I'm glad I answered," I said, then added when I caught up with myself long enough to remember my manners, "What's your name?"

"Alexa," she said. "Alexa McKnight."

"It's nice to meet you." I was beginning to feel embarrassed. Plagued by an out of control libido, perhaps I had gone too far.

"Would you like to meet sometime, Jameson?"

"You mean like at a hotel or something?" I asked, floundering.

She laughed. It was a warm, throaty sound that sent a tingle up my spine. "Actually, I thought dinner might be nice. We can proceed to other things if — and when — it suits us." Her voice was a low tenor, and brought to mind hundreds of movie maidens who speak in just the same way before succumbing to the charms of the hero. I didn't feel like a hero, but like a teenager, fumbling with my words and my proverbial zipper at the same time.

"Dinner would be great," I said. "When and where?"

"You pick," she said. "I like to get to know a man before inviting him for . . . other pleasures."

I hesitated, then, in a rush, "How about tomorrow," I asked, "Around seven?"

"That would be fine," she said. "Where?"

"There's a Greek café on the corner of 9th and Mitchell. They've got good food, and even better atmosphere. Do you like Greek?" I asked.

"Very much," she said. "Who doesn't like a good bite of Greek now and then?"

"It's called 'Sybil's Rock'. Do you know it?"

"I've never been there, but I'll find my way. I relatively new in town, but I'm starting to know my way around."

"That's great," I said, thinking that I was sounding more and more like a teenage boy whose dream date had just said yes to the prom *and* a midnight roll around in the backseat of his parent's car. "So I'll see you around seven?"

"Absolutely," she said.

"Good," I said. "I'm looking forward to it."

"So am I," she said.

"Wait!" I said, thinking she was about to hang up. "How will I know you? I don't have your picture."

"I have yours," she said. "And besides, I think you'll know me."

"Oh," I said. "Then I guess I'll see you then." Somehow, I could imagine her smiling, thinking I was a fool. "Good night, Alexa."

"Good night to you, Jameson."

As you might guess, I slept very little that night. I thought of Alexa, and the things we might do to — and for — one another the next evening. The short conversation replayed itself like a scratched record in my mind. I thought of Anaka — I had not physically been with anyone since her death — and I thought of betrayal. Would she approve of this strange, dark liaison? I didn't think so, and my separate thoughts of two women — one whom I loved, and the other I didn't know — stayed with me even in my dreams.

The café was dimly lit and pleasant, though it was busy. I had arrived a full half hour early to assure that we would have a good table. I sat in the semi-darkness watching other couples talk and sip shots of Ouzo. When she walked in, I realized she had been right. I knew her in an instant.

Her feet were clad in black leather ankle boots, and she wore black denim jeans that hugged her slender waistline. Her shirt was crème colored raw silk, open at the neck, and underneath, between the swell of her breasts, I could make out the faint lines of a dark purple, or perhaps red, lace brassiere. An embroidered black vest accented the outfit, and she carried a small, black purse in her left hand. I noticed her long nails, perfectly kept, and how flawless her hands seemed. Her neck was encircled with a slender gold chain and a locket. Her face was pale, and unblemished except for a small, circular birthmark just above her right eye. Her eyes were green — not the green of a forest glen, or a meadow in springtime, but the green of kelp washing onto the beach. And her hair . . . it was a dark, luxurious mane of red. It was a cigarette ember in the dark of night. It curled softly about her shoulders, a bonfire.

Her eyes met mine for the briefest instant, and she smiled. She was not what I had imagined on the phone, or while tossing and turning during the night . . . she was much more. As she made her way through the crowd, her eyes never left mine, and I did my best to appear composed. She walked effortlessly, somewhere (or so it appeared to my admiring gaze) between a glide and actual flight. The crowd seemed to melt away for her, clearing a path.

When she reached the table, I rose, and held out my hand. "You must be Alexa," I said.

She nodded, and set down her purse. "And you are Jameson," she said, taking my proffered hand lightly in hers, and clasping it gently.

"I am, and I'm pleased to meet you," I said, feeling a wild urge to kiss her hand.

"And I am pleased to meet you," she said. Her voice still carried that warm quality I had noticed on the phone.

I suppressed my gallant urges, and as we were seated, I gestured vaguely around the restaurant. "Will this be okay?"

"Oh, yes," she said. "Perfectly fine." She glanced around the room. "You were right about the atmosphere."

"I'm glad you like it," I said. "My wife and I came here often."

"You mentioned in your letter that your wife passed away a few years ago."

"Yes," I said, still feeling the guilt and grief from my thoughts of the night before. Seeing Alexa, those feelings were more distant, but there nonetheless.

"I don't wish to cause you pain, but may I ask . . ." she trailed off.

"Car accident," I replied. "Drunk driver. His third offense if you can believe it."

"I believe it," she said. "I'm sorry for your loss. How long have you been alone?"

"A little over three years," I said.

Just then the waiter arrived, rattled off the evenings specials, and took our drink order. I chose a bottle of

Red Zinfandel, and we waited in agreeable silence until he came back with it, and took our dinner order. Both of us selected the feature — a cucumber salad, lamb chops and pasta, with new potatoes. After he left, we continued our conversation.

"Has it been difficult for you?" she asked. "Being alone all this time?"

Fidgeting a little at the scrutiny, I said, "At first, I thought I would start over. Find love again, make the life-long commitment, but I've found that facing that prospect is asking too much of myself. It's been more difficult than I thought it would be."

"I find that hard to believe," she said. "You're the first person I've ever met through the personals who was honest about themselves and actually matched their picture. In the photo, you have dark brown hair, streaked with white, and lo and behold — in person you're the same. I suspected you were too good to be true."

I laughed. "So, you've had the experience of meeting someone through the personals who didn't quite match up to their description of themselves?"

"Oh yes," she said. "Quite a few times. I decided that it was pointless fooling around with the whole quest for true love thing. I hadn't really been getting anywhere."

"That sounds familiar," I said.

She smiled. "I understood how you felt when I was reading about you. I've been alone for a long time, too," she said, then added, "But isn't it interested how our feelings about love or lust can change rapidly from one moment to the next?"

"Yes, it is," I said. "You have me at a disadvantage, you know," I added. "You've read all about me, and I know next to nothing about you."

She laughed, lightly. "Just the way I like it," she said,

grinning. "It's good to have mystery in a relationship of any kind, don't you think?"

I nodded. "Mystery is fine," I said, "But that doesn't mean complete unfamiliarity. Tell me about yourself."

So she did. She said she had been born in London, but had moved to the United States with her parents when she was less than a year old. Her mother stayed at home, and her father was a professor of cultural anthropology at the University of Nebraska. There were no other children. She had grown up in a fairly normal environment, finished her Ph.D. in human biology, and then moved out to California for her work as a researcher.

While she talked, I watched her in growing fascination. Her voice, her gestures — they seemed uniquely understated, as though she were holding back a growing level of internal excitement. I couldn't seem to take my eyes off her hair, and I found myself wanting to reach out and touch it, to bury my face in its fiery softness and smell her perfume. When she finally wound down with her brief history, I felt disappointed as I enjoyed listening to her melodic voice.

"So," she concluded, "I guess that's enough about me for awhile. I haven't told anyone that much about myself in a long time." She shrugged. "Tell me something more about you. What do you do for a living?"

"Crosswords," I said, still distracted by the play of light in her hair.

"I beg your pardon?" she asked. "Did you say crosswords?"

"Oh yes," I said, then, seeing her confusion, I added, "I write crossword puzzles."

"I see," she said. "That's refreshing."

"How so?"

"Well, you just don't meet someone everyday who does that for a living. Write crosswords, I mean. Do you like it?"

"I suppose I do," I said. "I enjoy the challenge of constructing clues, and I've always liked word games."

When our dinner arrived, we paused our conversation long enough to get a good way into our lamb chops. Finally, she said, "So you enjoy word games? You must be well read then."

"Yes," I said, "Mostly personal ads."

And we laughed again. The rich warm sound of her voice cascaded around me, and I literally felt myself grow warm as I watched her. "You have a fine sense of humor," she said.

"Thank you," I said. "But in all seriousness, yes. I do read quite a lot."

This set off an entirely new discussion of different books and their merits. We ate, and talked, drinking the wine, and drinking in each other. By the time our coffee arrived, I somehow knew that I loved her. The poets speak of this phenomenon, but for me it was as real as any love I'd ever known. And though it seemed foolish, I found I was comfortable being a fool. It was senseless and fast, but she was, in every sense, a lady of intense qualities. It was also then that I realized I couldn't tell her my feelings. She actually deserved better than a one-night stand, and I suddenly knew that for all my recent cynicism about love and relationships, I had to respect her wishes about a relationship. She had been upfront about what she wanted, and it wasn't my place to try and make her change her mind. I felt a little like a child. I was a weak man who had fallen to his knees at the first sight of her qualities.

When dessert was over, the conversation slowed, and then stopped. I watched her, trapped between my desires for her physically, and the bitter knowledge that what I now knew I really wanted, I couldn't have. "Well," I said. "That was a fine meal, but your company was better."

"Thank you," she said. "You mentioned the excellent atmosphere, but I had no idea it would be this good," she added.

I smiled. "What happens now?" I asked.

"Now?" she said. "Would you like to take a lady for a walk along the pier?"

I nodded. "It would be a pleasure," I said, and I meant it. "Besides, I need to work off this baklava." I couldn't tell her no, and I knew I couldn't say yes to the implicit want in her eyes.

I paid our check, and we left. As we stepped out into the darkness, I took the liberty of taking her hand in mine, and in companionable silence, we made our way to the stone pier that borders the ocean.

*F*or a long time, nothing was said. We listened to the water lapping onto the shore, and the snap as it rolled over jetties of rock where people who couldn't afford real docks tied up their small boats. Occasionally, we would pass another couple walking along and enjoying the night. Orange colored arc sodium lamps provided the occasional island of light, but mostly there was darkness, and boat lights distant on the water that looked like stars. It was the most comfortable I'd been in years. Even though it was dishonest to continue on, I didn't want it to end.

Still, I was the first to break the silence. "Alexa, I've enjoyed tonight," I said. "Very much."

"As have I," she said. "More than I expected."

"Yes," I said, "Even more than expected. But . . ." I trailed off, looking for words.

"But?" she said.

"Well, I guess I've misjudged myself."

"How do you mean?" she asked.

"I thought I wanted I one night stand. Something purely physical, and by extension, something simple. But being with you tonight reminded me of all the reasons I loved Anaka, and I realized that I still want love, even more than I do sex."

She nodded, "I understand."

I was startled. "How so?"

She shrugged. "I find that I'm in the same boat. You see, I, too, lost my soul mate, and even though he isn't dead, I can no longer be with him. Being with you reminded me of him, much as you being with me reminded you of your late wife. I was wrong about what I wanted, and the only thing I can say is how happy I am that we're both in agreement of a sort."

I laughed, and she turned on me, a little hurt and angry. "This is funny to you?"

"No, no," I said. "Not at all. It's just that here we are, two adults dancing around the idea of sex, and both of us are thinking about love, and lost loves."

She smiled then. "You're right. There is something strangely funny about that."

"Look," I said, "I like you, Alexa. A lot. But I can't sleep with you because you deserve better than a one nighter with no commitments. I thought I was ready for something like that, but I guess I'm not, at least not with you. Maybe I'm not as cynical about love as I thought."

She softened visibly. "That's really quite sweet, Jameson. And spending time with you has helped me change my mind, too. Love exists, even for someone like you," she said, "Or me."

"Don't get me wrong, though" I added. "Alexa, I was watching you tonight, how the light played in your hair, the little gestures you make while you speak, and I hungered for the touch of a woman — but I want something more. Something permanent like I had before. I want to wake up every morning knowing that you're — excuse me — that someone's there."

"Someone?" she asked.

We were standing in a pool of that orange lamplight, and she turned towards me, her eyes upturned. "I want ... well, that is, I think that ..."

"Oh, shut up," she said. Then, with unexpected strength, she pulled my face down to hers, and kissed me. In the distance, the waves continued their rhythmic pounding of the shoreline, and somewhere in the city, church bells tolled the midnight hour.

W as it the bells sounding the midnight hour? Was it the passion of the moment, the way we seemed to join together in that instant? I still do not know. As our kiss deepened, the bells tolled, and I felt her lips tracing a small crescent along the line of my jaw and down to my neck. Then, a sudden pain as her entire body tightened — every muscle locked rigid, and she clasped me so strongly I thought my ribs would shatter. She held me this way for a few moments, and I could sense her struggling with something. Her lips moved against my neck, as though she were praying or nuzzling me. Finally, as though she could stand no more, she pushed me away.

"I can't," she said, so quietly that it was hard to hear her.

"I don't get it," I said. "You can't what?"

"I can't be with you," she whispered. She was turned away from me, staring out into the dark ocean, her body visibly trembling.

"I don't understand, Alexa. It's obvious you want to be with me."

She shrugged. "You don't have to understand. Just accept it. I can't be with you."

"Be fair, damn it! I want to be with you — you at least owe me an explanation!"

"I can't give you that, either. I'm sorry, Jameson." The bells had faded to silence, and over the waves, the city sounds resumed. "I've got to go," she said.

"Wait a minute," I said, grasping her shoulder and turning her around.

"No, Jameson!" she cried, but it was too late. I had seen her face.

Her eyes were now the color of blood, even in the orange light I could see they were red. Her skin looked vaguely feverish, and pale, though she had appeared healthy enough earlier. But the worst was her teeth. They had grown! They were so long and pointed that her canines jutted down past her bottom lip.

"What the . . ." I said, before she quickly turned away.

"So," she said. "Now you know."

I was dazed. "What do I know?" I asked. "That you aren't who you appear to be?"

She laughed, and now it was a grim sound, full of old disappointments. "You like word games, Jameson. You've seem me, you saw my ad, what am I?"

Still reeling, I tried to piece it together. Her ad said she wanted a one-night stand. What was so significant about that? And then it hit me — all at once, and I was stunned I hadn't seen it before. Her box number . . . when you signed up for the personals service, you selected your own box number. Mine, 9673-626 spelled out 'word-man' on any standard phone pad. Hers, 8267-473, spelled vampire! Her ad had said that the respondent must "understand the hungers of the flesh." I put a hand to my head, which was suddenly aching.

"You're a vampire?" I asked. "A vampire?"

"You really are good at word games, Jameson," she said. Then, "Yes, I am a vampire. And now you know why I can't be with you." She was still turned away.

"A vampire?" I asked again, still floundering.

"Yes!" she half-screamed. "A vampire! You know, a blood-sucker. Creature of the night. The whole thing."

Feeling like my head was buried in cotton, I tried again. "Why are you dating?" I asked.

She spun around, and I took a not-so-involuntary step backwards. "Do you think that being a vampire is proof against loneliness?" she hissed. "Do you have any idea how long forever is?"

Taken aback, I gestured vaguely around. "I . . . I guess not. How the hell would I know, anyway?" I asked, annoyed. "I'm standing here having a conversation with a vampire. Either that or I'm cracking up. It's not like you take a vampire to dinner every . . ." I trailed off as a thought struck me. Vampires don't eat dinner. "Wait a minute," I said. "Vampires don't eat, right? What'd you do with your food?"

"Simple illusion," she said. "One of the few benefits of being what I am."

"How did you . . . oh, never mind," I said. Then another thought struck me. "You weren't looking for a date, were you?"

She turned away again, but I could hear her response. "No," she mumbled. "Not really."

"You were going to *feed* on me, weren't you?" I asked, nearly shouting myself. "Jesus Christ! Do you do this often? Let guys take you out to dinner and then drink their blood?!"

She didn't answer, and that was answer enough.

"So, this wasn't a date, wasn't even cheap sex. It was how a vampire hunts in the modern age, right? Everything you told me was bullshit."

"It's not like that," she whispered. "Not really."

"Then what's it like," I snapped. *"Really."*

"It's a little more death every day," she said softly. "Always aching to be alive again, to feel something besides the hunger — and always being denied. It's too late to lie to you, and I don't really want to anyway." She turned back to me, and for a moment, I saw *her* again. Not the monster within her, but the real woman trying to escape. "You're right, of course," she said. "Everything I told you before about me, who I am, was a lie. A necessary lie, but a lie nonetheless. And usually, this is how I feed. I hate it, but that's a hunger that cannot be denied. Some desperate soul responds to an ad that appears to be for sex, he takes me out and then I feed on him. It's not pretty, but it gets the job done."

"Then why didn't you feed on me?" I asked. "I'm pretty desperate. In fact, you might say that death would be a blessing."

She nodded in understanding. "For many of them, it is. But for you . . . I couldn't do it. That's just it. When I read your letter, and then I met you in person, I thought that . . . well, I thought that you might be the one. And when we kissed, I knew for sure, and that's why I pushed you away — before it went too far."

"Before what went to far?" I asked.

She pointed at my neck. "Touch yourself," she said, "There on your neck where I kissed you."

I did, felt a small wound, and pulling my hand away, I saw blood. "You were sucking my blood?"

She nodded glumly. "Yes," she said. "But I stopped in time. You may feel a little weak for a short time, but that is all. I stopped because when I tasted you, the essence of you, I knew you were the one."

"The one what?" I asked.

"Even vampires can love," she said. "Isn't there a saying that there's someone for everyone? Well, it's essentially true, but in the case of a vampire it's more than basic. It's part of the deal."

"What do you mean?"

"I mean that all vampires have soul mates. We don't run around making other vampires. We only make other vampires out of our true soul mates — sometimes a good friend, more often, a lover. Some vampires find theirs right away, while others search for years before finding the right person."

"So you're lost love is a vampire, too?"

"Oh yes," she said, bitterly. "And that's why I have to go now. He's coming here, this night, and I can sense him drawing closer to me."

"But why would you leave?" I asked. "If he's your soul mate, why can't you be with him? I would give anything — anything at all — to have my Anaka back."

"Because he's not who he was then. He's become a true monster, feeding on those he chooses without regard. 200 years ago, he was nearly killed by a mob of peasants, would be vampire killers, outside of London. He was horribly scarred, physically and emotionally by the ordeal. He lost his love of the world, and those in it, and slowly, I lost my love for him."

Thinking on this, I felt a little bad for her. "What about you, Alexa? How long have you been alone, looking for another soul mate?"

"Most of the last 200 years," she said. "But who's counting?"

"Will I become a vampire now?" I asked, a little frightened.

"No," she said. "It didn't go nearly far enough. I stopped in plenty of time."

"I'm flattered, I guess," I said. "It's not everyday that one meets a vampire who thinks you might be their soul mate." I paused, thinking, and added, "That is that what you meant when you said you thought I was the one, isn't it? That I am your soul mate?"

"I haven't changed my mind, Jameson," she said. "You *are* my soul mate."

"But I can't be a vampire!" I said.

"Not yet," she said.

"Not yet?" I echoed.

"I can tell you're not ready yet. Not ready to make a true commitment. This is a true commitment, Jameson. There's no turning back, no divorce. It's forever and ever, amen." Then she added, "I don't mean us per se, because even soul mates can lose their way in the darkness. Love can fade and people can change. I mean becoming a vampire. There's no turning back into a human."

"I think you're wrong, Alexa. I'm ready for a commitment, but not this fast and not this sudden. And I don't think I'll ever be ready to be a vampire."

"You will one day," she said. "I can see it when I look at you. I can taste it." She turned, scanning the pier with her eyes. "He's coming closer, now. You must go."

"I think your wrong about me, Alexa. If you think I'm destined to be your soul mate — to be a vampire for God's sake — then fine. But I'm glad you didn't turn me into a vampire or kill me. This is just way too much, Alexa, and way too weird. Thanks for an interesting night." I turned, and began walking down the pier. For some distance, I was alone with my morbid thoughts.

"Jameson, wait!" she cried, running towards me.

I turned. "What is it?"

"It wasn't my choice, you know," she said. "To be a vampire."

"I didn't assume so," I said. "Who would choose that?"

"You'd be surprised," she said. "But the point is that the vampire who made me didn't ask, or give me a choice. He simply said, 'You are one of us' and made me what I am. He was a good person, but he had no sense of timing and certainly no subtlety. I'm giving you the choice I didn't have."

Looking at her then, with the city and ocean sounds surrounding us, I almost said yes. Part of me wanted to scream yes with all my strength. But I couldn't then, and I could sense her fear, too. Whatever her maker had become, it scared her. And if it scared a vampire, it must be quite horrible. Her observation of me had been correct. I wasn't ready for an eternal commitment, not really. And I certainly wasn't ready to face a scorned lover from her past, who happened to be an angry vampire. "I'm sorry, Alexa, or whatever your real name is. I can't. Not now, and probably not ever."

"I understand," she said. "But one day, you'll change your mind."

"Maybe," I said.

"Love is funny that way," she said. "Once you feel it for somebody, once the fire has begun to burn, there's no turning back, only turning away. Sooner or later, your heart leads you to find that person again, and to warm yourself next to whatever flame they will offer."

"Maybe," I repeated.

She tensed slightly, and I could see her fangs once more. "I have to go now," she said. "The hunger grows. It's long past time for my dinner. I will lead him away from here, and you. I can sense your fear." She began walking away, when she stopped and looked back at me. "We are connected now, Jameson. When you are ready, I will know it, and we will meet again."

And with that, she walked away. Her long red hair flashing like fire in the lights along the pier. I watched her until I couldn't see her anymore, thinking about what she'd said. Thinking how cold it was at home with no one there and nothing to comfort me but old memories of a wife three years in her grave. Thinking that she was probably right — sooner or later, I'd want to be warm again.

I returned home, alone, and wondering.

*T*wo weeks later I saw him for the first time. I was walking home from a late night walk to the corner store for ice cream, and I saw a man who had once been quite attractive, but now bore the scars of someone who had been in a horrible fire. He walked behind me for some distance, and I waited, trying to control my urge to run, certain that at any moment he would pounce on me, perhaps drain my body of blood and leave me lifeless on the pavement, a bizarre headline for the following day's newspaper. Finally, with my heart racing, I couldn't stand it any longer, and I turned to face him, only to find myself alone on the sidewalk. With my breath rasping in my throat, I made my way home.

That night, I wondered how long it would be before we actually met. His intention, no doubt, was to confront me, perhaps kill me, so that I could no longer be of interest to Alexa. Had he found her that night, I wondered? I didn't know for sure. I had long since realized that Alexa was right about one thing. I thought about her constantly, and was soon searching for her along the pier, and once, I accosted a red-haired woman who was perfectly human — and quite startled by the madman grabbing her and calling her Alexa.

Sometimes, during quiet moments alone, it seemed as though we were connected, that I could feel her inside of me. I wondered where she was, if she was safe from the machinations of the monster that now stalked me. I wanted to talk to her again. To watch the light play in her hair like little children made of fire. How had he found me? Was he watching us that night from some great distance? Could he feel her, as I seemed to?

For another month, I watched for him. Sometimes catching the merest glimpse of his shadowed form in the distance. Once, I thought I saw him staring through my window, but when I looked closer, I saw only my reflection. Seven weeks after Alexa had gone, her lost soul mate and I met, though not in the way I had expected.

Shortly after sundown, the doorbell rang. When I answered it, he was there. The scarred face I had seen earlier stared in at me, and I jumped backwards, holding up my hands to ward him off.

"Stop," he said. "If I meant to harm you, no force in the world could stop me." His voice carried a vague accent, and was quite deep.

My pulse was racing. "What do you want from me?" I asked.

"Nothing you will not freely give," he said. "You have already — in a sense — done what I desire. I merely wish confirmation."

"Why have you been following me?"

"To see what kind of man you were," he said, and then gestured into the house. "May I come in?" he asked, "So that we may speak as civilized beings?"

"I've done my homework, vampire," I said. "You cannot enter here unless you are invited."

He smiled, and stepped into the entryway. "Not everything you read is accurate, fool. A writer, even one such as yourself, should know that. I was being polite."

I nodded. "Okay," I said. "Come on in, as it seems I cannot stop you."

He stepped the rest of the way into the house, his

long stride carrying him past me and into the living room. He was quite tall, and moved with easy grace. His hair was long and black, and tied into a ponytail with a length of dark silk. Turning back to me, I saw that his eyes were dark blue. "Why don't you sit down," he said, "and we can talk."

I sat in the wingback chair I preferred and gestured him into the other. "Alright, talk," I said.

"You are a direct man," he said. "That's good. I find it refreshing."

"I think we can dispense with the compliments and polite necessities for the most part," I said. "What do you want?"

"Your word," he said. "Your word that you will not pursue Alexa. She is mine, for now and eternity."

"I think you're mistaken," I said. "She is her own. You can't own somebody like that. Love doesn't work that way."

"I think your opinion of such matters is of little value. I made Alexa, when your long dead ancestors were still trying to fight off the natives of this land. I have loved her from the first, and she has loved me. She cannot deny that. She mustn't."

"For someone as old as you apparently are, you haven't garnered a lot of wisdom in those years. Love is something that cannot be permanent by its very nature — it takes work and sacrifice, it is built on those foundations, not on a flimsy foundation of want or desire. Like any fire, if you leave it untended long enough, it will go out."

"So, you're wise enough to instruct me in the ways of love between immortals? Bah! Alexa doesn't understand me. That is all. She thinks I am some sort of monster, when all I am is a realist. Humans despise and fear us. Caring about them will only get us hurt or killed, because sooner or later, humans — who are no more than animals that walk upright — will strike out at that which they despise and fear."

I was frightened of him, then. Truly scared. Not because he could kill me, though that was scary enough in its own right, but because he saw us as animals. And when you see something as an animal, it usually has less value in your eyes than others of your own kind. I thought of Alexa, and I knew why she had left this . . . thing disguised as a man. "What is your name?" I asked.

"My name?" he said. "What does it matter? Give me your word, and I will leave you in peace. You will not see me — or her — ever again."

"Your name, please?" I said again. I was still thinking of Alexa, and then I could feel her. Somehow, I could feel her as though she were in my arms, and I felt safe.

"Don't be foolish, human," he said. "I do not like games."

"This is no game," I said. "Your name — what is it?"

"Very well," he said. "My name is Demetri Vasile."

"Okay then, Demetri Vasile, I'm Jameson Servais, and I cannot give you my word."

He looked at me then, and I watched in that slow moment as his eyes turned from their dark blue color to the icy blue of arctic frost. He hissed. "Do you wish to die, fool?" he asked.

"No," I said. "I don't. But I'm not a liar, and I won't append my name to a lie. I love her, which is more than you can truly say, having kept her away from everything she's wanted for two hundred years. She was right, you are a monster."

He leapt to his feet then, and I was certain that he would reach out and kill me with one blow. His fangs were bared, and I found that his eyes, which had changed again to become the color of blood, impaled me. "Then you've made your choice," he snarled, reaching towards me.

When Alexa spoke from the doorway, he froze in amazement. "Demetri! Stop!"

He turned to her. "Alexa!"

And then it happened, so fast that I barely saw it. Her arm whipped forward, and a long wooden spike flew across the room and buried itself in Demetri's chest. He howled, an animal sound of rage, and pain, and love finally broken and betrayed. I stood, stunned, as she crossed to his writhing form on the floor. He tried to pull the stake out, and couldn't seem to find the strength.

"I'm sorry, Demetri. You don't know how sorry. But now it's truly over, as it should have been years ago. The stake is barbed, and you cannot remove it. In a few more moments, all the years you have cheated death as a vampire will return for you, and you will be nothing but a withered husk that will blow away in the night wind."

He looked up at her then, and I could suddenly see the man he'd once been. "Alexa," he said. "Why?"

"Because you are no longer my soul mate," she said. "The bond is broken." I felt a strange internal snap, and the connection I felt with her grew even stronger.

"You cannot!" he said. "To be soul mates is to be together forever."

"You are not who you were," she said. "I'm sorry."

His struggles slowed, and age lines began to appear on his face, wrapping around the scars from that long ago bonfire. "I love you, Alexa," he whispered.

She shook her head. "No, Demetri, you don't. Or it never would have ended this way."

Suddenly, his whole form stiffened, and he howled in anguish one last time. Alexa and I stood silent, while the returning years took their terrible toll. Finally, he fell still, and his clothing collapsed in on itself. Nothing remained but the cloth, the stake, and a few pieces of bone.

She turned to me, then, tears the color of blood tracing paths down her face making a bizarre compliment to her hair. I wrapped her in my arms and held her, very glad to be alive and with her once again. "I loved him once," she said. "Long ago."

"I know," I said.

For nearly half an hour we stood just like that. Our arms around each other, knowing that the storm was over, and wondering how we'd managed to survive. Then, she gently pushed me away. "I have to go," she said.

"Why?" I asked. "I want you to stay. I was wrong before. I am ready."

She smiled at me then, and took her hand. "No, Jameson. You weren't wrong before. You're not ready for this yet. I didn't destroy Demetri for you, or even for us. I did it for me, and even for him."

"I love you, Alexa, but I guess you know that."

"I do, Jameson. And I love you, too. But you need more time to truly accept what becoming a vampire means. I'm giving you the time."

I didn't say anything, realizing she was right. For the first time since Anaka had died, I was truly glad to be alive. I nodded in acceptance, and said, "You won't forget about us, will you?"

"No," she said, softly. "I will be waiting for you, and when the time is right, I will come and we will be together." She reached down and gathered up what was left of Demetri. "I have to go now. It's getting late."

I nodded again. "When will I see you again?"

"When it's time, Jameson. When you are ready."

I kissed her then, once, softly, and I could see that this was not easy for her either. "You're right," I said, wanting to make this easier for her, maybe even easier for me. "I'm not ready yet. But I will be one day, and on that day, I want you to come for me. We can be warmth for each other."

"You are already my fire," she said. Then, quietly, she left.

And when I knew for certain she was gone, I sat down in the wingback chair, put my head in my shaking hands, and cried.

Many long months have passed since that night. And I think I'm almost ready now to face what being a vampire really means. Sometimes, I can feel Alexa nearby, so I know she is watching over me. Does she keep me safe from whatever other creatures hunt the night? I do not know.

Of course, I don't read the personals anymore — there is no real need, even for the grim amusement I might feel once again, now that I have found love. At night, I lie in my cold bed and wonder if this will be the night she comes. I wonder if she is not also waiting to be ready herself, if the wounds she must have felt when she destroyed her lost soul mate Demetri have begun to heal? Those wounds will heal, in time.

And we have a long time. I can wait for her, though I am impatient to hold her, wrap her long hair in my hands and taste her lips. When we are both ready, she will know it. She will come to me in my darkened bedroom, my angel of death, and love, and lust. When that night comes, whatever warmth she brings, I will welcome her. I will bear my throat to her gentle fangs. And we will consummate our relationship with a kiss a midnight, in blood the color of roses, the color of her hair, the color of fire.

Printed in the United States
16832LVS00001B/324